VIKING GOLD

Book Two in the Carswell Adventure Series

L.A. SARTOR

To Jim
with thanks
for all you're doing
for me
LASartor

Print Edition

Viking Gold is a work of fiction. Names, characters, places and incidents are products of the author's imagination or are used fictitiously. Any resemblance to actual events, or persons, living or dead, is entirely coincidental.

eISBN: 978-0-9856792-8-6
ISBN: 978-0-9856792-9-3

Printed in the United States of America
www.lesliesartor.com

"After all, what is the purpose of finding these artifacts if one can't enjoy them? It would be like owning jewelry that one didn't wear or art one didn't display."

~ Hermann Weiss

Dedication

For my aunt Leslie. I'm incredibly proud to be her namesake. She was outspoken, exceedingly generous and extremely good at whatever she attempted. She always seemed fearless to me and did what had to be done. I hope to have half her grit and determination. I wish you were here to celebrate the publishing of my fifth book with me. I miss you every day.

To my mom, Mary Sartor, who has always believed in me and who proofs each manuscript with amazing care, a feat for someone suffering with macular degeneration. You are a heck of an inspiration forever.

And as always for my darling Gary who has learned that I can get lost while writing and not hear him. Sorry, babe. Now he simply makes a note and talks to me when I've left my book world. I love you.

Acknowledgements

No writer I know works alone. Yes, we sequester ourselves as we write, be it in coffee shops (too noisy for me) or in our offices or at our dining room tables, but there are people we turn to for advice and help. These are my treasured compatriots. I thank you all.

Audra Harders, an incredibly talented writer in her own right who offers not only to always be my beta reader but just happens to be my best friend.

Amanda Cabot, a prolific and wonderful writer whose opinion I deeply value. I count on her vast experience to find plot inconsistencies and character missteps.

Ellis Vidler, my editor who always makes me a better writer. Thank you doesn't begin to cover my gratitude. I know I couldn't do this without your help.

Colonel Michaël Svejgaard, Royal Danish Air Force (ret.), who helped me enormously with the correct information on the Luftwaffe aircraft, forms and airbases which he has researched through original documents and photos for the past thirty years. Colonel Svejgaard served as Chief of Staff, Joint Operations Forces, Denmark. He is the author of the book *Der Luftnachrichten Dienst* about the German Luftwaffe's night-fighter command-and-control network in Denmark during WWII. And he's incredible at Google-Fu and found answers to my obscure questions.

Sven Gust who sent me pictures of the fjords in Norway and its creatures—specifically Trondheimfjord. He generously read my dive scenes to make sure they were correct. He works as dive guide for Northern Explorers AS, Norway. He has about 2,500 dives in Norway and the Arctic under his belt. Over the last ten years, Sven worked as a scout and support diver for several film teams making documentaries about the unique underwater world of the Trondheimfjord. See pictures at http://www.lasartor.com

Dr. Jane Kershaw for so kindly sharing her amazing research on Viking Metals. Jane is an archaeologist at University College London, specializing in Viking-Age Britain and Scandinavia. She keeps a research blog on aspects of Viking-Age metalworking.

Gunnar Klippenvåg Sørum archivist at The Regional State Archives of Trondheim, took pictures of the inside of the archives and sent them to me on a cd. I hope I did justice to the rooms and the building.

Dr. Svein Carstens took the time to send me historical as well as modern pictures of the old Nazi subbase Dora-1. His kindness changed my story's direction. He is a historian, archivist, researcher, writer and teacher. In addition Dr. Carstens works for the real estate company DORA in Trondheim where, among other things, he has contributed to establishing a regional archive center. He has been doing historical research since 1988. He earned a Doctorate in medical history and is employed as a professor at the regional University College. He-is researching humoral anatomy.

Chapter One

"You should have caught the bouquet. I threw it right at you," Victoria Carswell said as she led the way into their familial home on the cliffs of the Oregon coast. The laughter from the reception guests and the music from the jazz quartet followed them into the house.

Abigail Carswell grinned at the touch of pique in her sister's voice. Abby wasn't going to play that game and had deliberately bent to fiddle with her shoe the exact moment Tori tossed her spray of lilies, white roses and ivy.

"BJ needed it more than I did. Didn't you see the glow on her face after she caught it?" Abby said as she followed Tori, her older twin by a mere two minutes, into the intimately familiar bedroom they'd shared until their thirteenth birthday.

Closing the door, Abby leaned against the smooth, cool oak, immediately soothing her overheated skin but not her overfrayed nerves—caused by her uncharacteristic foot-dragging, not the hot June weather.

"Why are you being so stubborn about

marrying Hermann? You adore him, and we could have had a double wedding."

Tori's bewildered tone matched the confusion Abby had been dealing with for the past year, ever since Hermann Weiss had gone down on one knee and asked her to be his partner in all things. To be his wife.

Joy and giddiness had filled her as he slipped an exquisite three-carat, yellow diamond solitaire on her finger. She loved this man with a fierceness that stunned even her.

It was only later in the evening that Abby had felt the first pangs of uncertainty, and anxiety. Even Hermann noticed. She'd seen it in his eyes, but bless her German, he had said nothing, instead choosing to hold her tight.

When Tori announced that she and Reid were getting married and asked Abby and Hermann if they wanted a double wedding, Abby saw the joy in Hermann's eyes. But it was quickly doused when she said she wasn't sure if the timing was right.

Of course it would have been right, if only she could rid herself of what was stopping her from committing completely to Hermann.

Abby let loose a sigh. "Would you believe me if I said I don't know why I'm hesitating, or as you put it, being stubborn?"

"Oddly, yes," Tori said. "But still, you're the more adventurous one. And marriage is definitely going to be an adventure. So I expected you to dive in right along with me." Tori pirouetted in the tight space between their old twin beds, still covered in the same African quilts their parents brought home from one of their adventures long ago.

The strapless, sleek column of her sister's cream-colored wedding dress hugged her body until it reached her knees, then swirled with an abundance of sheer lace twirling at her feet. Watching her sister, Abby forced a smile, wondering what Tori would think about her secret name for the dress: Super Barbie Gown.

The day matched the radiant joy Tori exuded. It was still hard for Abby to believe that only a year ago, Tori had been timid and reclusive, living on a train. Designing jewelry for some of the most famous people in the world, but never socializing with any of them

Tori designed 14-karat gold headbands studded with gems for them to wear. Her own was very bridal with diamonds and pearls, and Abby's was covered with rich golden topazes, chocolate and white diamonds. Tori wore her hair upswept with the headband glimmering in the curls of her dark hair. Abby chose to keep hers loose, held back by the band.

It just felt better to have it unconstrained . . . unencumbered.

She shook her head ever so slightly, frustrated by her tangled emotions. They only had a few private minutes to get Tori dressed for her honeymoon, and Abby didn't want to waste it feeling the hollowness deep in her soul when

"Hermann" and "marriage" were in the same sentence.

She wondered more than once if there was something wrong with her. Maybe she needed counseling. But how could she explain to anyone else what she herself couldn't vocalize?

"Help me with the zipper, okay?" Tori asked, bringing Abby back to the moment.

Abby pushed away from the coolness of the door, immediately causing the persimmon-colored silk of her maid-of-honor gown to stick again to her hot, moist skin.

She worked the zipper on Tori's dress, inching it down the side as her sister raised her arms. "Any idea yet where Reid is taking you?"

"Nope. I just know it's not Mexico."

Letting loose a laugh, Abby hugged Tori. "Seen enough of that, eh?"

"Maybe forever."

Their gazes met and held as a frisson of remembered fear passed between them. Tori almost died saving Abby in the Yucatan, more than once in fact. But she'd come back stronger in mind and body.

And Tori fell in love with Reid Hunter, her total opposite. He'd been in Mexico to find a mythical jade artifact, Tori to rescue her.

Once Reid had been Abby's partner. They'd parted ways and from that point on had been rivals seeking the next great treasure.

"Well, there are a lot of beaches in the world

other than Mexico, and I'm sure Reid has picked the best for your honeymoon," Abby said lightly, trying to remove the memory of that experience from this day of celebration.

Tori's bag was already packed with the trousseau Reid had requested. Bathing suits and shorts. That was it. Reid kept the location a secret, but obviously it had to involve sun, sand and water.

Weeks of sun. Abby swallowed her sigh. It was just what she needed.

Although today was hot for June, the early weeks of the summer had been foggy, damp and chilly—the traditional June gloom of the Pacific Northwest. She needed the sun and surf to bake away the sense of uneasiness, and some beach drinks to remind her she was still carefree and could even be silly. Mexico had taken away a lot of that.

"Meine Lieben, the limo is in the driveway." Hermann's voice boomed through the closed door.

"My loves?" Tori whispered.

"You're like a sister to him," Abby whispered back. "Hermann, less than five, okay?" she called loudly as she tugged the snug "Barbie gown" over Tori's hips, creating a puddle of cream silk on the floor.

True to her word, Abby opened the door in just under five minutes, admiring the duo of men who stood waiting. Hermann's white blondness, the strength of his chiseled chin, the gentleness and love in his gaze. And Tori's Reid, dark hair with a pirate's glint, a cocky smile and his lucky fedora.

Abby handed Hermann a small suitcase and moved aside so Tori could step out.

"Ready, Darlin'?" Reid asked, pulling his bride against his chest and capturing her lips with a kiss, a long deep kiss.

"Save it for the honeymoon," Abby teased. It still amazed her that Tori could blush so readily; she couldn't remember the last time her own cheeks turned pink.

Hermann linked her arm in his, and they followed the newlyweds out of the house and into a shower of birdseed thrown by the guests lining both sides of the walkway.

The chauffeur took Tori's bag from Hermann and stored it in the trunk as Abby hugged her sister one last time. Hermann clasped Reid's hand, and the men exchanged a wink. Abby gave him a questioning look as he came back to her, receiving a bland smile in response. They were up to something.

Which was proof once again that the distrust the two men had harbored since the China incident several years ago had disappeared. Reid's stubbornness finally gave way when he asked Tori to marry him and realized it was important for her sake that both Abby and Hermann had no doubts about him. Finding the men to corroborate his story took a lot of work. Then between Hermann and Reid's various methods of persuasion, the men were convinced it was in their best interests to tell the truth.

The stretch limousine drove slowly around the tight curve and down the long length of the paver-laid driveway. The car was still being pelted by the last of the birdseed as guests chased after it. Then it was gone.

The quartet in the garden that curved around the side and back of the house struck up the music again, and people drifted back to dance and enjoy the rest of the reception.

Abby didn't move from her spot even after the limo was long gone from view.

"Today has been tough, ja?"

Abby pulled her gaze from the empty driveway to smile at her fiancé, knowing she couldn't hide the tears in her eyes and realizing it was okay. This was Hermann, the man she loved and had pledged her heart to. She moved into his open arms, always finding his embrace a safe harbor. "In the best possible way."

"Which means perhaps, you are finally softening to the idea of actually going through with our marriage?"

"Herr Weiss?" A voice interrupted them.

Saved by the bell. Abby, flooded with guilt over her unworthy thought, turned in Hermann's arms to see a twenty-something man shouldering a backpack, wearing shorts and a T-shirt, with lines of fatigue bracketing his mouth.

"Ja."

"It appears I've come at an inconvenient time."

He nodded toward the sounds of the reception still going strong. “But I must talk to you, today if at all possible.”

***

Using the caution that had become second nature to him since his own twenties, Hermann closed the sturdy French doors to the office in the Carswell house. He motioned for their uninvited guest to sit in one of the leather club chairs while he chose the chair directly opposite for himself. Facing the man made it easier to spot nervousness and any signal of falsehood or danger.

And the younger man was nervous. He'd set his backpack between his legs as if for safekeeping, and he kept wiping his palms along the khaki fabric of his shorts. Hermann noted his backpack was a leather Hermès, his shorts were Arc'teryx and his T-shirt Armani. He either had or came from money.

“Thank you for—”

Hermann held up his hand to stop the young man from completing his sentence. “We wait for Abby, please.”

Their guest looked around the room that was once the office Abby's parents used to plan their archaeological digs.

“This is quite an office, Herr Weiss,” Sigurd said.

Hermann looked around, trying to see it from the younger man's perspective.

The elder Carswells’ lives had been dedicated

to finding treasure that was said to be unfindable. To prove, as Hermann did now, that there was nothing hidden that couldn't be found.

This past year, with Abby's permission, Hermann had recreated the room so it worked as a joint office for the two of them. Additionally there was a small partner's desk for Tori and Reid if they ever needed it while working at the Carswell homestead.

Hermann felt for the first time that this house could be a home. For him and Abby to set down roots. For Tori and Reid, it would be the place they could always come home to.

"Don't you worry that the treasures in the cases are at risk of being...stolen?" Sigurd motioned to the wall of display cases that held the Carswell and Weiss treasure finds.

Hermann continued his perusal of the room. The treasure cases, secure with bullet resistant glass and his latest laser alarm system, lined one wall. Additionally, the windows in the room were one-way glass, and when a curious guest asked, explained away as a shield from the hot westerly sun.

Rich mahogany bookcases filled with classics and pulp fiction lined the other two walls. But the real magic of Hermann's empire lay secreted behind the cases in a room with all the gadgets and high-tech communications gear he so loved and used to create the Weiss empire.

Not many people were allowed to visit this

room, and had it not been for the wedding reception, this man wouldn't have been here.

"Not at all. Everything in here is very well protected," Herman said. "After all, what is the purpose of finding these artifacts if one can't enjoy them? It would be like owning jewelry that one didn't wear or art one didn't display."

"I agree."

Hermann noticed the gleam in the young man's eyes, and realized it wasn't from what he saw before him, but from something he wanted them to do for him. And this room filled with treasures was evidence he'd found the right people.

A few more minutes passed and Abby entered and, as Hermann had, carefully closed the door behind her. "The caterer and Alfred will keep everything running smoothly until we return."

She glided across the room, the persimmon gown swaying gently around her curves, and perched on the arm of his chair. *God, she was stunning,* Hermann thought for the millionth time. Abby was beautiful in shorts or cargo pants, but the color of the gown, the flash of the gems in her hair and with his diamond on her finger . . . she looked regal.

"Tell us why it is so important that we have this conversation right now," Hermann said, keeping his voice pleasant but neutral.

"You're the only person I know who can solve this mystery."

Hermann felt Abby's glance, knowing it held a

glint of amusement at the man's dramatic choice of words. Motioning for him to continue, Hermann waited, watched and listened. He'd been right; the man did want something from them. But what?

“Sorry, I should introduce myself. Sigurd Thorsen, student of Trondheim University, Doctoral Candidate at the department of Sociology and Political Science.”

Hermann nodded. He'd pegged him as Scandinavian from the accent, even with the darker hair and green eyes. Not all Norse were blond and blue eyed. The Vikings traveled to and settled in many parts of the world, and Hermann was fairly certain Sigurd had more Celt in him than classic Norse.

Sigurd again wiped his palms on his khaki shorts. “My research and dissertation regard the plundering of cultures, ancient and current, and how such activities continue to rob subsequent generations.”

Sigurd's gaze lifted from Hermann's to take in the shelves of artifacts behind him.

Hermann couldn't read the expression in the young man’s face. But the closest he could come was knowledge, as if he knew far more than he was telling them.

Odd and disturbing.

“As you know,” Sigurd continued, “Norway wasn't exempt from Nazi occupation. I've been sifting through hundreds of communiques, and one wreck in particular caught my eye—”

"Herr Thorsen, dozens if not hundreds of ships have been sunk on Norway's western shores."

"Yes," Sigurd answered with a shrug. "But this isn't a ship, it's an airplane. And it ditched or crashed in the narrows of the fjord between Stadsbygd and Ingdalen, west of Trondheim."

"Fjords are too deep to dive safely."

"Agreed, but I know you have a Remote Underwater Vehicle."

How did this whelp know that? While it wasn't a secret, it wasn't common knowledge. "And you want to rent it?"

Hermann wasn't expecting laughter, and the younger man's chuckle took him by surprise.

"No, sir, I want you and Ms. Carswell to find the treasure, bring it up and give it back to the people of Norway."

***

Treasure?

From her perch on the arm of Hermann's chair, Abby glanced down at him in time to catch the surprise, then the gleam in his eyes, which he quickly masked, but which echoed her own feeling.

For the first time in a year, a sense of purpose, a pulse of excitement coursed through her. Yes, this was what she needed, a new challenge to tackle.

And marriage wasn't challenge enough?

Once again Abby pushed aside her guilt over not making that final commitment. "What treasure?" she asked, careful to conceal the excitement in her voice.

"Before my father died, he gave me a piece of gold, telling me his grandfather had stolen it from a secret Nazi operation. The only other information my grandfather would give my father was that someday all the treasure would come back to the people because the gold wouldn't stay in Germany to line the pockets of the bastards."

Abby nodded. "That's a good story, but—"

Sigurd held up his hand, then carefully pulled a slim, worn leather-bound book from his pack, opened it, flipped through some pages and handed the opened book to her.

In a niche cut into the yellowed and brittle pages nestled a section of exquisite, intricately wrought gold. Abby picked up the piece, feeling its weight and warmth, carefully noting it was about three by two inches and about ten millimeters thick. Running her finger lightly over the interwoven design that the Norse craftsmen were known for sent the familiar rush of a new adventure through her. "Viking gold?"

Sigurd nodded.

"It's beautiful, but it will need to be tested for authenticity."

Sigurd dipped his head in agreement.

Reverently, she placed the small treasure back in its niche and passed the book to Hermann. He, too, held the gold with utmost care and respect, then nodded as he looked at the backside of the gold.

"Tradition runs deep."

Abby looked at Hermann. "Explain, please."

He held up the gold piece, pointing to the faint lines scored into the backside. "Payment during Viking time was frequently made in metal, silver more often than gold. Gold was turned into jewelry, which could be turned into payment. The Vikings were very exact in their measurements, so it wasn't as if they hacked off a hunk of gold and used it. They knew exactly the value of each centimeter of the metal."

"I researched my father's claim as it fit in with my own thesis and I found items that corroborated his story. Now is the time to find this gold. And if it is as my great grandfather said, then it is a part of our legacy and should be seen and cherished by the people of Norway."

Something about Sigurd rubbed Abby the wrong way. His arrogance she could dismiss as nervousness because he wanted something from them. But there was another layer to him she couldn't pin down. It wasn't merely that he'd interrupted a celebration, or that he was arrogant. She mentally shrugged, knowing she and Hermann would talk about all this after the younger man left.

Abby turned her attention back to the conversation.

"That's an altruistic statement," Hermann noted. "And it wouldn't hurt your Doctoral candidacy either."

"No, it's merely the truth. We should be proud

of our heritage. Vikings were savage but also established law and governments. Wagner's opera started the horned helmet syndrome, as I name it. It's an unfair portrayal. We are a proud nation. And yes, it wouldn't hurt my candidacy. It's, as you say, a win-win situation."

"Why us?" Abby asked, patting Hermann on the arm. His hand covered hers, his thumb running lightly over the inside of her wrist. It was an intimate gesture, and as always, it left her a bit breathless. He'd touch her face as he kissed her, or wrap an arm around her shoulder as they watched the sunset over the ocean. It didn't stop him if people were around, and frankly it still surprised her that her stoic fiancé had such a romantic side to him.

"Because you two are what I need. I've compiled quite a dossier, fact and . . . fiction."

That was an odd thing for Sigurd to say. And she wasn't sure why he chose to look directly at Hermann, holding his gaze for a few seconds.

Hermann's fingers tightened on her hand, and she'd bet he didn't realize he'd done it. More to talk about after their guest had left.

"You both had family involved in archeology and treasure hunting, and you both lost parents due to that fascination. And while you, Ms. Carswell, either work for yourself or the highest bidder, Herr Weiss works not only for the pure joy of discovery but to prove his father's innocence—"

"I don't want to be rude, but we do have

guests." Hermann slipped the gold piece back into its niche and held out the small book to Sigurd.

Abby's excitement deflated instantly. Hermann had just indicated he was in essence done with the conversation and most likely the hunt.

Sigurd couldn't have said anything worse. She didn't know all about Hermann's father, but she did know that something continued to trouble him about how he and his brother had died. To this day, when every one of Hermann's new engineering inventions was certified, he'd rejoice and drink a toast to the reputation of his father and brother.

The accident in which they'd died had been the big news her parents had talked about with Alfred Choy, the twins' tall inscrutable Chinese caretaker when their parents were away on one of their adventures.

He'd taught them how to wield a butterfly sword and made sure they learned martial arts. To be still and listen to the world around them. To find answers when other people had given up.

And when their parents were home, Alfred would leave on his own mysterious jaunts. Never revealing—at least to Tori and her—where he'd been.

It was on their parents' last visit home that they'd talked about the elder Weiss's accident. Apparently Alfred knew about the legendary sword and the area Hermann's father was searching in. Abby had only been twelve at the time, and had lost interest in the adult conversation quickly.

Eighteen years later she'd worked on a team with Hermann and fallen head over heels in love with him. Searching the Internet one day for a piece of equipment she thought would be useful on a quest she and Hermann might want to join, she unearthed an article about that fateful dig. Hermann's father had been an engineer and an archaeologist, and had died while trying to find the tunnel that led to the famed diamond sword buried somewhere in Vietnam's massive Son Doong Cave.

When she asked Hermann about the disaster, his response had been so typical for him. “Liebchen, it is the past, so we shall let it remain there, eh?”

Abby figured everybody grieved in their own way, so she did as he asked. But obviously it wasn't in the past, as Hermann's toasts to his father attested, and Sigurd had just touched a nerve.

He ignored Hermann’s gesture of returning the small book by keeping his hands in his lap. Abby couldn't help but admire his moxie. Most people wouldn't do that to Hermann. Despite her disappointment that her fiancé flatly rejected this adventure, she was intrigued to see what would happen next. A huge part of her hoped Sigurd would be able to reestablish the glory of the hunt and Hermann would be once again intrigued.

“Of course. Forgive me for being less than considerate to you and your guests. I chose you, Herr Weiss, because you have the tools, the equipment and the experience. Going through government authorities and getting funding takes time, and who knows what will happen when the gold is found? It may end up locked in a vault. In that case, nobody gets to enjoy and learn from this heritage.

"We"—Sigurd's gesture included all three of them—"will work privately, and the treasure, when found, will go toward the greater good. Once again, Herr Weiss will be known as one who has found the impossible."

Hermann said nothing for a few beats. Abby wanted this adventure, but she wasn't going to tip the scales, so she bit back the words and held her breath.

Hermann put the book on his thigh. "As Abby mentioned, we'll have to test the gold first. Will you leave it with us?"

Abby breathed. Hermann was softening.

Sigurd held Hermann's gaze. "As long as it doesn't leave your protection."

"Naturally. We have an x-ray fluorescence machine here."

"Then test it. When would you like me to return for your answer?"

"Give us a few days. You have a way for us to reach you?"

"Here is my cell number." Sigurd handed Hermann a business card and rose, shouldering his pack.

Hermann handed her the book. She wanted to

caress it, open it and hold the gold. Let her imagination run to the world of the Vikings, the people, the mystique. But she needed to wait until she was alone.

Abby watched with wry amusement as Sigurd stuck out his hand to Hermann first, only changing direction after Hermann nodded ever so slightly in her direction. Apparently not all European men had her fiancé's sense of chivalry.

Hermann deliberately followed Sigurd out of the room, firmly closing the door behind them.

After locking the door, Abby lifted the gold out of the book and held it. She felt the story behind it and knew without a doubt this was an adventure they had to follow.

Nestling the gold back into its niche, Abby had to make sure the book was safe until Hermann tested its hidden treasure. She had no doubt the gold was authentic, nor did she suspect Hermann doubted it. But she knew he'd conduct the tests. He lived for this kind of hunt.

Thankfully Sigurd had used the right words: “found the impossible.”

Abby stood before the wall of bookcases smiling wryly at the titles Hermann picked this week, and pushed the two books forward in sequence: *Pride and Prejudice* by Jane Austen, and *Cecilia* by Franny Burney, a book Abby wanted to read. Hermann had chosen romances in honor of Tori and Reid's wedding. Who knew what he'd choose for next week's code?

The bookcase swung aside noiselessly, revealing a huge vault door.

Quickly working the combination on a small electronic keyboard—a tricky passage from *Moonlight Sonata*—she put Sigurd's book with its precious cargo on one of the shelves. Abby closed the vault door, which automatically locked it, swung the bookshelf closed and went outside to mingle with the guests, hoping none of them would ask why she didn't have a double wedding with Tori.

Alfred was in deep discussion with Dr. Hysing of the Chinese Archaeological Society.

Abby wondered if Alfred was aware of how frequently he massaged his shoulder, wounded so badly during the hunt for the Stone of Heaven last year in that surprise attack by the Immortal's minions last year.

He turned toward her as if reading her thoughts, a slight frown marring his ageless face.

Alfred briefly touched the area of his heart, knowing without needing words that she was fretting. She was surrounded by people who loved her, yet she still felt adrift, without purpose.

Maybe this new adventure would help settle her.

Viking gold. An unbelievably rare find.

Chapter Two

The morning after the wedding, Abby opened one eye to see the sky burnished with the gold and pink of early dawn. They were going to have another day of glorious sun.

Scooting across the wide bed to snuggle with her love, she patted the lump of bedding she thought was concealing Hermann only to find it was the down duvet in a jumble. He must have slept badly, for typically it was her side that ended up in a tangle of blankets.

Abby pulled on shorts and a T-shirt, drew her hair into a ponytail then padded down the stairs to the office sure she'd find Hermann there. Empty.

In fact, neither Hermann nor Alfred was in the house, and Alfred wasn't supposed to leave for another few days on one of his many mysterious jaunts taken this past year. As was so typical of him, he offered up no information about where he was going or why.

She and Tori knew better than to ask. Reid was still cautious around Alfred. Only Hermann could get away with questioning the twins' mentor.

Abby headed out to the patio, nodding absently to the cleanup crew as they packed away chairs and tables from the reception that had lasted long into the evening.

She walked onward to the edge of the cliff, scanning the sand below, hoping to see either Hermann or Alfred. At the farthest edge of the beach's cove, Hermann sat alone on a bleached and gnarled tree trunk, elbows on his thighs, his chin resting on clasped hands. He faced the sea. But she'd bet he didn't see any of the beauty before him.

Something about Sigurd's visit yesterday really bothered him. Hermann was quiet after the last of the lingering guests left the reception. His brooding wasn't directed at her refusal to set the date for their wedding; it was as if Sigurd Thorsen's visit had touched a deeply buried nerve.

Most people wouldn't have noticed, but Abby saw the tightening of his fingers, the deceptively calm tone of his voice, the spark of a new challenge—deliberately tamped down as Sigurd talked. An awareness passed between the two men. A knowledge of some sort not welcomed by Hermann.

It was time to talk. The secluded beach, a perfect spot.

Abby quickly headed back to the kitchen and filled two insulated mugs with coffee. Then she went back to the cliff's edge, and with both hands full, carefully planted each foot on every one of the four dozen steps down the gray and weathered wooden staircase that zigzagged to the beach. She needed no twisted ankles or broken bones if they might indeed take on this adventure.

Kicking off her flip-flops, she crossed the damp sand, dodging piles of seaweed and tangles of driftwood. The tang of the salty air filled her lungs and her soul. There was a freedom to the ocean she connected with.

Why couldn't she be content simply being here with the man she loved?

Abby paused before joining him. As always, whenever she was lucky enough to capture a stolen moment to study him, she couldn't believe this handsome man was hers. His profile was classic, chiseled perfection. She itched to trace his jawline, which invariably led to him nibbling on her finger, then pulling her into an embrace that seared her soul to his.

"A penny—"

He whirled around as if he hadn't sensed her approach. Peculiar, as Hermann possessed catlike instincts and was rarely taken off guard.

"My thoughts aren't worth even a penny."

"You got up early this morning, even beating the party's cleanup crew."

"I didn't sleep much."

"I know."

Rising from his perch on the log, he took both mugs from her, then he bent and twisted them into the sand so they'd stay upright. He straightened and pulled her into his arms, holding her tightly.

That stunned her. Hermann was always attentive, the most amazing lover, always making sure of her pleasure . . . but this embrace felt different. Almost as if he was afraid of losing her.

"Sigurd—" they said simultaneously.

"Go ahead," Abby offered, needing to know what felt so wrong about Sigurd and his request of them.

"I started analyzing the gold last night—I can't quite pin it down. It doesn't seem to be melted and reworked gold, as was much of the later Viking gold. I thought at first the principal source for this was likely late Roman and early Byzantine gold coins. Its alloy is close to but not quite the same as the Dumfries and Galloway hoard, which, from the latest research, was from around 900 AD. This gold seems more pure."

"But?"

"If it is as this Sigurd says, then indeed this find would be a coup on his part to return it to the people of Norway."

"But?"

"I've done a quick background search of Sigurd's family. They weren't wealthy until the war. If they had this gold piece prior to the war, which he seemed to suggest when he said his father's grandfather had stolen it back from a secret Nazi operation, I'd expect them to have moved in much higher financial circles."

"His family were sympathizers and he's feeling guilty?"

"I haven't gone that deep yet. But I did wonder about the guilt as he was nervous—or acting that way—when he first came to us. It could all be a fabricated story, and he happened to find the wreck info when he was researching for his thesis and wants us to help him. He'd surely have a great dissertation then. Anyway I've got good people on it—"

"You called Reid this early? It's three hours earlier in Hawaii."

"No, I texted him with a buzzer to go off at 10 a.m. So we have a while to wait, which is okay as there is no one better than he is on searching out obscure anythings."

She shook her head and smiled easily. Amazing what difference a year made in their relationship. A year *and* proof that Reid hadn't intended any harm to come to Hermann in that botched China event.

"So what's bugging you?" She reached up and smoothed the frown that marred his forehead.

"Am I that transparent?"

"Only to me. You cut Sigurd off ever so politely when he started in on your history. I got the sense you don't really like him."

"It's not a matter of liking him. Something isn't feeling right and I can't nail it. So we make no decisions until I find out what's bothering me."

Abby stilled her fingers on his brow at his emphasized "we." She knew it was because she hadn't conferred with him when she'd gone after the Stone of Heaven in the Yucatan, and it had nearly cost all of them—including Alfred—their lives. And although his “we” chafed more than a bit, she knew Hermann was right. They were a couple and needed to decide as such.

If only she could let that happen.

Abby felt Hermann's focus shift to something far away from this moment. He'd done it before, and it hadn't bothered her, for it was usually an engineering problem where a solution presented itself.

This time was different; it felt like she was closed out. But bugging him wouldn't do a bit of good. In fact it only increased his stubbornness.

She slipped easily out of his embrace and sat on the log, waiting for him to return to the moment. Pulling her coffee mug from the sand where Hermann had placed it, she sipped and let the scent of the dark brew, the acrid taste combined with the tang of the ocean, and the endless rhythm of the tide soothe the rough edges of her irritation. It wasn't her nature to be patient, be thwarted, or denied a secret, and apparently Hermann had at least one.

She knew about his immense wealth. He was brilliant at engineering new concepts. He handpicked a team of engineers at his plant in Darmstadt, Germany. His equipment had been instrumental in saving Reid and Tori's lives in the Yucatan. He sold his designs to governments, individuals and other engineering firms. Some called him a genius.

And she thought so as well.

Abby didn't know much about his past loves and didn't want to. She knew little of his childhood, but that lack of knowledge wasn't an issue. She didn't know if he had a close relationship with his mother. He never talked about her, and his father and brother were off limits.

Well, she had a few off-limit subjects as well, and Hermann didn't pry, so for the moment she'd take that page out of his book and be patient.

Minutes later, Hermann refocused and sat beside her. As she studied his face, she handed him his coffee. He had the same haunted and distant look in his eyes now as when she'd brought up the mystery surrounding his father's death.

The excitement over the prospect of another grand treasure hunt suddenly dimmed and left her with a hollow feeling. If Sigurd Thorsen was resurrecting something in Hermann that caused pain and angst, then this adventure was best left alone.

Full circle, her thoughts came back to the "we" Hermann had used. "I think *we* need more information regarding Sigurd before *we* can figure out what's bothering you. And for some reason I have my doubts as well, but I can't put a voice to them." She touched his arm, feeling the warmth of his skin. Deep, nearly overwhelming love coursed through her. "I want you to know, this adventure isn't worth any amount of the angst you're going through. So think about giving him back the gold and saying goodbye."

Abby waited a few beats to see if he'd agree. Instead she got a long, studying gaze from him before he turned back to look at the sea.

She rose from the log, bent and touched her lips lightly to his, then headed back to the house to let him be alone with his thoughts. Even though she wanted nothing more than to have him open up to her and tell what the issue really was.

Nobody could make Hermann do that.

Not even her.

***

Hermann watched Abby slowly cross the sand of the cove, stop to put on her flip-flops, then climb the long wooden flight of steps up to the bluff and home.

Home. It was here in a house not owned by him that he finally felt he could allow roots to grow, to create a home. Not in Germany, not in Paris or Mexico where he owned houses that he rarely slept in. It was here in Oregon with Abby.

And it rankled that she wouldn't commit fully to him. But moments ago, she'd repeated twice his own use of the word "we." Maybe he was making some headway with her. And she loved him enough to offer up a major concession by suggesting they not take on this adventure.

When Abby reached the top of the bluff and disappeared from sight, Hermann turned back to his study of the sea. He hadn't felt the past creep into his life so vividly since he'd met Abby and fallen so completely in love.

Perhaps he'd read too much into that one phrase Sigurd uttered about still needing to prove his father's innocence. But if the younger man had really done the exhaustive research he said he'd done, he would have realized that long ago Hermann proved his father's innocence to those who defamed his family. Not only had his father's tool worked to fabricate an exo-skeleton as support while it excavated a tunnel, but in test after test, in conditions worse than Viet Nam's Son Doong Cave, the tool worked flawlessly.

Twenty-one years ago his father and his brother had set out for Viet Nam to find the fabled diamond sword. Hermann, twenty-two, had wanted desperately to go with them, but it was his last semester at the Technical University-Munich and he was being inducted into the honorary fraternity of engineers, which his father felt was far more important.

When the news reached him that his only family perished and the fault lay with his father's design of a new digging tool, Hermann knew the reports of the faulty tool were false. He tried to outshout the liars since he'd helped his father design and test the equipment and knew it to be innovative *and* sound.

When nobody listened, Hermann took the last of his father's wealth and built every tool that his father had designed for the company. He proudly labeled them with the family name, but because his father wasn't there to see them built, it was an empty victory for Hermann.

Then Hermann designed and built hundreds of his own inventions, innovating equipment far ahead of the curve and turning Weiss Engineering into the engineering equivalent of Apple or an Elon Musk enterprise.

He fought for and created every ounce of respect he'd garnered.

He no longer needed to prove anything to anyone.

Nor had he given up the dream of finding the unfindable. Hermann had always enjoyed watching movies about lost treasure, from the oldies like *King Solomon's Mines* or *Atlantis, The Last Continent* to the Indiana Jones series, knowing that most of the audience thought the stories simply a good romp. He knew better.

As he knew, there were both archaeologists and treasure hunters, and the line between them was often so blurred as to be indistinguishable.

While he wasn't a scientist of archeology, he still loved the respect that came as a reward for finding something known only in fable and myth. Pride was also the point of view Hermann's father had held.

And then there were the treasure hunters. Those who wanted the celebrity and wealth from selling the finds. His Abby was one of those. Reid Hunter as well. And while Abby or Reid wouldn't kill for an object, they'd fight hard to get there first.

Hermann's brother, Peter, had also been one of those, and had often argued with their father over choosing the dig that had the most potential for money or prestige versus the excitement of simply being the one who'd found the unfindable.

Gulls screamed above, catching the wind, pulling him out of his reverie.

Maybe he was simply being too sensitive to Sigurd's choice of words. He thought he'd put to rest the need to prove anything more, either about his father or himself.

He'd agreed to test the gold, and when the fluorescence X-ray had confirmed that the gold was at the very least Viking era, the appetite for this hunt increased.

He knew Abby wanted it. Not only was Viking gold incredibly rare, the fact that it might be Nazi plunder increased the stakes. Add in the one peculiar element in the gold he couldn't identify and he had a search that would be rewarding.

Hermann forced himself to relax and let his mind concentrate on his breathing. A form of meditation, quick and effective.

But not this time. After ten minutes, he realized he needed to meet with the young Norseman once again and see if he was still bothered enough to call off this quest.

Pulling out the card Sigurd Thorsen had given him, Hermann flipped the thin card between thumb and forefinger and noticed a poorly erased name on the backside.

Bayside Bed and Breakfast.

***

"*We* need to go together," Abby said, standing in the garage with her arms crossed, not willing to take no for answer. "After your reaction to Sigurd yesterday and your pensiveness today, I want to see his response to *us* showing up—"

Hermann leaned forward and captured her lips in a quick kiss. He pulled back and flashed her a slight upward curve of his lips.

Damn the man. He had a way of taking all the spine out of her. Abby re-gathered her thoughts, "And if the plan is to take him by surprise and gauge his reaction, my car is the better one to take," she finished, breathless.

Hermann simply nodded.

They slipped into her new toy, a low-slung, black BMW i8, and as it was electric, she soundlessly backed out of the garage.

The sleek car made short work of getting to the Bayside Bed and Breakfast. She pulled onto the expensive crushed granite circular driveway and realized the B&B was pricey, well above the means of an average grad student. This, combined with his high-end clothes and equipment, added one more element to the mystery that was Sigurd Thorsen.

Stopping the car well away from the front door to keep their approach under Sigurd's radar, she and Hermann left the car, quietly closing its doors, and surveyed the Bayside Bed and Breakfast. The house, painted a soft dove gray trimmed in white, stood a slim three stories tall with a one-story glass conservatory attached to the side. Something about the place pulled at her, but she couldn't pin it down.

The blue-painted front door was open, so they entered, and within moments were met by a spry woman Abby guessed to be in her early seventies.

“Abigail Carswell, it's good to see you again. I bet you don't remember me, but I knew your parents well.”

“Really? You should have come by the house and reacquainted us. I've been home for about a year now.”

“Oh, I did, about six months ago, but you weren't in. Someday I figured we'd meet again. You and your sister, Victoria, used to clam down on our cove. Remember?”

And suddenly Abby did. That was what had pulled at her.

She remembered getting cut by those razor clams while competing against Tori to see who'd reach their maximum haul first. Later, Alfred would make a savory chowder, and they'd eat on the broad porch. If their parents were home, they'd drink wine with their chowder and tell the best stories about their digs.

“Mrs. Bottomsworth. Of course.” Instead of extending her hand, Abby wrapped her in tight hug. “I'm so sorry I didn't remember in time to invite you to Tori's wedding. Will you forgive me?"

"Only if you and your handsome man come to dinner at the beach some evening," she said, eying Hermann.

"My fiancé, Hermann Weiss." Abby quickly made the introduction, and loved the way Hermann charmed Mrs. Bottomsworth, being completely sincere as he admired her inn.

"So, we're here to see one of your guests. Sigurd Thorsen," he finished.

"Oh, yes, I just took coffee out to him. Odd young man, but—"

Abby quirked a brow, waiting for her to continue.

"Oh, my, I can't be gossiping about my guests now, can I? He's out in the gazebo. If you want, I'll bring a couple more cups."

At Hermann's nod followed by a wide smile, the lady strode away. "I like your Mrs. Bottomsworth."

"And she you, apparently," Abby whispered back.

They headed out through the wide, opened glass doors of the conservatory.

The white wooden structure perched near the edge of the cliff was as charming as the main house. Sigurd sat facing the sea, a laptop in front of him on the glass table. They couldn't have asked for a better scenario. He certainly wasn't expecting anyone. If he had been, he would have faced the pathway. Or at least that's what she and Hermann would have done.

Hermann steered her onto the grass, avoiding the noise of the crushed gravel path that would alert Sigurd to their approach.

They got to the steps of the gazebo, and Abby could just make out part of a Celtic symbol on Sigurd's computer screen. Closing her eyes, she committed the partial image to memory. She'd draw it on paper the moment they were alone, then send it to Reid and see if he could come up with its meaning.

Hermann cleared his throat, announcing their presence.

Sigurd slammed down the lid of his laptop and spun around, haughty anger twisting his face.

Abby winced for the machine's screen, instantly aware the image was something Sigurd wanted hidden. All the more reason to find out what that symbol meant.

“Herr Weiss, Ms. Carswell, I didn't expect you—”

“I hope it's not an inconvenience that we're here?” Hermann asked smoothly. “After all, you scribbled the name of your accommodations on the back of your card.”

Abby fought her grin. Hermann was so good at staking ground in a conversation.

“No, not at all. I'd forgotten I'd written it down. I'm surprised you stopped by today. I thought testing the gold would take longer. I hope this means you've made your decision,” Sigurd said.

Abby admired his quick comeback, which neatly covered his extreme reaction.

At that moment, Mrs. Bottomsworth appeared with a tray, cups, another carafe of coffee and a plate of scones. After placing the tray on the table, she left, but not before sending a smile that bathed Abby in a sense of being home.

“Do you mind?” Abby pulled out a chair. Sigurd waved a hand in her direction, obviously still discomfited by being taken unaware.

Abby poured a cup of coffee for herself and one for Hermann, handing it to him.

“May I ask how you intend to pay for the use of my ship and equipment?” Hermann asked.

Abby hadn't seen that question coming. She sipped her coffee, ready to enjoy the verbal sparring.

“Herr Weiss, I know your research ship is berthed in England, so I figured it wouldn't cost much to get it to Norway. And as I said before, I know you have a Remotely Operated Vehicle and are developing a new Autonomous Underwater Vehicle as well.”

Sigurd wasn't as meek at he was yesterday, as if he'd baited the hook and thought he'd already caught them.

Abby watched Hermann's expression, seeing irritation pass across it, then, as yesterday, a grudging admiration.

“And I guess you assumed we would pick up the costs of the salvage as well?”

"Yes, to be able to give the people of Norway their heritage back. To find and expose Nazi theft. It's the new hunt de jour, you know."

"Which makes no difference to us. What will you provide?"

"The location, the permits, and the crew. The information."

"We have our own crew. The permits will take months, and summer is the only time to do this work. The location . . . " Hermann shrugged as if that weren't valuable enough information to bargain with.

"Herr Weiss, I would not have brought this to you if I didn't have permits in process. We can start immediately."

Hermann sipped his coffee while looking out at the ocean. Abby could sense the wheels churning in his mind. Weighing the pros and the cons of taking on this adventure.

She'd already made up her mind. She needed to go, needed this as much as a writer needed to write, a singer to sing. But she wouldn't if Hermann was still bothered by something.

The silence was killing her, but she kept her mouth shut, waiting for a signal from Hermann. She felt Sigurd's impatience as he picked up a small crumb from the scone on his plate and crushed it into dust.

"Is there nothing more I can say to sway you to make up your mind today?"

Abby felt Hermann's glance and met it

squarely, putting as much affirmation as she could in her eyes. She nodded once ever so slightly, but it didn't matter as Sigurd paid her no attention.

"As you said, the ROV is ready to go. The AUV," Hermann shrugged, "isn't quite ready, but I'm quite sure I can borrow one from the University in Trondheim. I've worked with them before. And there may be two associates joining us."

Abby breathed a silent sigh. She didn't want to take on any quest without Reid and Tori coming along, or at least offering them the chance to be a part. She should have trusted Hermann to do it right. *Yes, you should have. Come on, girl, give the man a break. You love him, so stop trying to find issues that prevent you from committing fully to him.*

"Then I can give this to you now, a gentleman's agreement not to pass on the information." Sigurd handed Hermann a packet of papers.

"Except to our associates, of course." After Sigurd's nod, Hermann passed them to her.

She carefully opened them, and on top was the copy of a yellowed Nazi document with faded white teletype-like strips that appeared pasted to it. "Es-o-s, Es-o-s, Es-o-s, Explosion, NHAD, Notwasserung in 06 Ost 94632," she read.

Abby handed the note back to Hermann. "Translate, please."

"Mayday, mayday, mayday, explosion, NHAD, ditching at 06 East 94632."

"NHAD?"

"The plane's call sign, unique to each one."

The next sheets were copies of old black and white photographs of jewelry, trinkets, coins and other ancient items of metal. The photos looked as if they'd been burned or trashed, and it was hard to tell if all the trinkets were gold, but there were at least a dozen pictures and they were all different. If this is what they were after, they'd best move quickly. Once the news got out that this was available, there would be poachers.

"Where did you get all this?" she asked as she passed the pictures to Hermann.

"As I said, I combed through hundreds of documents, mostly from the state archives in Trondheim. I can give you the file number if you are questioning the authenticity of the document. The photos I found in my father's things. They were heavily damaged, so I made copies of them."

He looked away as he mentioned the photos, perhaps in guilt that his family had obviously taken part in something sinister or heinous. But his tone implied the opposite of his body language. Superiority.

Abby nodded. "Yes, I would like that."

"I am not offering what I believe you call a wild goose chase."

"We wouldn't have agreed to one. As we tested the gold, we'll verify the documents. Do you know where the photographs were taken?"

"As I said, I found them in my father's files at home after he died, in a box marked for destruction. I have no idea where they were taken."

"Odd he didn't tell you about them."

Sigurd shrugged. "I was amazed he told me anything, let alone gave me the gold piece. We weren't close."

Hermann looked up from his study of the photographs. "This is an extremely valuable hoard."

"Which is why I felt it was imperative to come now, even though I interrupted a wedding. Time is short."

"I understand and agree with your haste."

"I'll book the tickets then," Sigurd said.

"First Class at least for Abby and me. We prefer Lufthansa and SAS. Use Mrs. Johnson in town; she has all my information. It's Sunday but here is her home number." Hermann handed Sigurd a phone number precisely written on paper from a small notebook he always kept with him, whereas Abby could rarely find a clean scrap of paper in her purse. "I promise you, she won't mind the call." Hermann held out the packet of photos to Sigurd.

"Keep them, I have copies at home."

Abby got up, not expecting a handshake, and she didn't get one.

She tried to quell the building excitement, then figured why bother. This is what she lived for. They needed to pack, talk to Tori and Reid, and see if Alfred wanted to join this as well. The whole family could be a part of this. And that thought pleased her tremendously.

Preceding Hermann to the car, she saw Mrs. Bottomsworth in her lovely herb garden. "Mrs. Bottomsworth—"

She looked up from deadheading the lavender. "Goodness, call me Mary."

"We're heading off but expect to be home in a month or less. And we'll get together, I promise. All of us, including Alfred. Remember him?"

A red stain crept up the older woman's neck and onto her cheeks. Mary brushed back her hair with a gloved hand. "Of course I remember Alfred Choy. I would love to see him again as well. Do you have someone to keep an eye on the place?"

Abby wondered about Mary's blush. "Yes, thank you, it's all taken care of." Hermann had sensors all over the house, and a gardening staff for the yard. Yep, everything was taken care of.

"Then, dear, have a safe journey. Until you return."

Abby was saluted with a handful of lavender and realized for the first time that coming home wasn't going to be a letdown. It would be good.

But not as good as finding Viking gold.

Chapter Three

Tori stretched out on one the many chaises on the lanai as the waves of the Lanikai beach on the windward side of Oahu gently lapped the shore.

Reid had done good. The flight was long but not as long as other tropical isle destinations would have been, such as Tahiti for instance. And she didn't mind a bit that they were staying in a house Hermann had asked them to scout out for possible purchase.

Hermann would love the place. Gadgets for the gate, the curtains, the door locks and probably more they hadn't yet discovered. A blue-tiled pool that ran the length of the crushed shell driveway, where a row of multicolor ti plants provided privacy for a skinny-dip. And the beach-side lanai where she was currently relaxing . . . well, it was to die for.

Teak planks formed the deck, with a low wall of dark gray volcanic stone separating the broad swath of wood from the grassy area that melded into the beach and ocean merely yards away.

The same volcanic stone surrounded the massive fire pit at one edge of the lanai, circled by benches covered in rich tangerine and greens. Huge pots with ti plants dotted the deck, which offered cozy seating areas and an outdoor gourmet kitchen.

Where Reid was grilling two steaks. Deciding she needed to be closer to her new husband, Tori swung her legs off the chaise, snagged her glass and the bottle of champagne, and crossed to his side. Topping off his glass, she waited until he flipped the tenderloins. Then she wrapped her arms around his waist and was rewarded with a searing kiss.

"Darlin', I think if Hermann doesn't buy this house, we should," he said with a smile.

"It's pretty perfect."

"Could you give up your train?"

Tori thought for a moment. She knew living on a train wasn't what Reid had expected, but he loved it. They'd bought another rail car and had it outfitted to house their BMW convertible. When the train was stationed, they would drive around investigating whatever town they were near. She still had her studio car, and Reid had converted Alfred's railcar into his office and private sanctum.

"Honestly? I don't know if I could live on an island full time, but for a second home, wow. And I really don't want to give up *our* train."

"Glad to hear it. I'm becoming quite fond of moving around the country in ultimate comfort."

Handing him his champagne flute and watching the man who captured her heart take a sip, his gaze never leaving hers, a tiny shiver ran across her shoulder blades at the memory of those horrifying moments in Mexico. Thinking she'd lost her newfound love before she even had the chance to tell him.

"I'm not leaving you ever, you know."

"Mind reading again?" Tori asked lightly.

"No, but I can always tell when you think about Chuca or Tulum. You change, go still, and the light leaves your face. And you're still having nightmares, though you try and hide them from me. You don't need to—I'm here for you always."

Tears welled in her eyes and spilled over. "God, it's our honeymoon and I'm crying," she said, swiping at them.

Reid cupped her face and thumbed the tears away, then captured her lips again. Until the sizzling of the steaks and the growling of his stomach pulled her back.

"I love you, Reid Hunter. For now and for always."

"And, Tori Darlin', I love you. And I'm looking forward to a long married life, filled with love and adventures."

She bit her lip again, holding back the tears. She was the luckiest person in the world.

Reid plated their steaks and led the way to the glass-topped table. Holding one chair back for her, he seated her and then placed the napkin in her lap.

"I hope madam is happy with her steak. If not, the chef will eat it for her."

"Not a chance." And it was true. They tucked into their dinner, accompanied by baked sweet potatoes, followed by mango sherbet they'd found in the freezer.

Sipping coffee and watching the sun begin its descent, they snuggled on one of the oval loungers built for two with its own canvas lid, and watched the waves gently roll onto the shore. At this moment, Tori felt the world held only the two of them.

Until the chirping of Reid's cell phone intruded.

"It can go to voice mail," Reid said.

"Maybe it's Hermann wanting to know if we approve of the house."

"Then let's tell him no, and we'll buy it."

Tori punched him on the arm as he rose to grab the phone from the kitchen counter inside.

"Aloha, Hunter residence."

Tori smiled as he walked back out, phone to ear. It had to be Abby or Hermann on the line, otherwise she was sure he wouldn't have picked up.

"Whoa, wait a second. I'll put the phone on speaker. Tori's right here."

Reid mouthed "Abby" as he sat on the lounger. "Okay, it's on."

"You're on too. Hermann is here. When are you going to learn to use face-to-face so we can see you?"

"I know how to use it—it's our Honeymoon remember?" Tori teased. "We might not want you to see us, got it?"

"Got it," Abby said, getting the words out between guffaws of laughter from Hermann.

"Reid, did you have any time to check on the Thorsen family?"

Tori still heard the laughter echo in Hermann's voice.

"Yep, he's got an interesting family tree. His great grandfather, Hadrid Thorsen, was some sort of underling for Josef Terboven, who was Reichskommissar for Norway—"

"Reichskommissar? What is that? Sounds like a Nazi something."

"Bingo, Abby," Reid said. "Reichskommissar is a Reich Commissioner, in this case for the occupied Norwegian territories. And he used the GSSN, which was the Norwegian branch of the Germanic SS—a mostly non-military branch—for imposing Nazi doctrine. I haven't yet found Hadrid's rank in GSSN. Anyway, prior to joining that group, Hadrid was a member of Nasjonal Samling, a political group that used expressions and symbols from Norwegian Viking traditions."

"Then Sigurd's nervousness, his defensive attitude all make sense," Hermann said.

"Why?"

"Tori, I think he's embarrassed that his great grandfather was part of that group. All the more reason to find the gold and give it back," Hermann said. "He'd almost be a national hero. And there might be a bit of remaining dislike for Germans in general. Yet if I'm the best, then he needs me. German or not."

"Gold? Needs you? Norway?" Reid repeated, excitement dripping from each vowel. "The Kattegat fjord wreck? It's real?"

Tori groaned. Reid had wanted to find that shipwreck since last year. She shivered. Norway was synonymous with cold, made especially obvious when she was sitting outside in tropical warmth with an idyllic beach right in front of them.

"Not that wreck, Reid. A 1940s airplane filled with Viking gold that was plundered by the Nazis."

"Okay. That's good too," Reid said with a wink at Tori.

"We're heading to Norway tomorrow," Abby said. "And I know this is your honeymoon, but we wanted to offer you a chance at this gig—after all, we're a team."

"We'll be doing some diving, but most of the deep water work will be done with the ROV," Hermann added.

Tori looked at Reid, one brow raised in question.

"Remote Operated Underwater Vehicle," he whispered.

Tori raised both brows. "Sounds expensive. Hermann, I don't suppose you have one?"

Hermann's chuckle on the other end of the call

made her laugh. "Okay, silly question."

"So we called," Abby said, "to see if you wanted to join us."

Tori saw the excitement bloom in Reid's eyes, and a quiver of the same raced across her back. He met her gaze and held it for a moment.

"It's a long flight, Darlin', are you sure?" he whispered.

She nodded.

"Okay then, how about we meet up mid week?"

"Works for us. This will be our first foursome," Abby said.

"Excellent," Hermann said. "I'm sending your phone a dozen photographs of what we believe to be the hoard, a transcript of the plane's SOS call and the quadrant map where we think she went down—"

"And Reid, I'm sending a symbol I'm unfamiliar with, but I know you'll work your magic and figure it out."

"Always my pleasure, Abby."

"Is Alfred coming?" Tori asked.

"Ja, but later. Probably after you arrive. He's on another project. Reid, even though we're set to work with Sigurd, see if there is anything more about his great grandfather."

"You got it."

"See you both Wednesday then. Auf Wiedersehen."

"Wait. Hermann, buy this place, or we will. It's totally awesome."

Again Tori elicited a chuckle. “Perhaps we should buy it together, eh?”

“That is one hell of a good idea. One for all, all for one. Meanwhile, onward to the gold,” Reid quoted and reached for her hand, squeezing it tightly.

Tori felt Reid's excitement and matched it. No bad guys this time, only retrieving the gold alongside her twin and Hermann, whom she loved like a brother. Tori hoped Alfred would be there soon as well.

One big happy family.

Chapter Four

From his room's window on the top floor of the inn, Sigurd watched the tide sweep in, as inexorable as his destiny. To be part of a world where men as smart as he was controlled those who *thought* they ruled the world, like that German, Hermann Weiss. Playing among those who used the sword or the pen, playing out in front of the world's eye, making themselves appear to be powerful.

Sigurd knew better. The true warriors of today worked silently, shaping power, playing the leaders as pawns, using force when necessary, not afraid to do so, never seeking the world's approval or needing the limelight to posture their position. Those were the men and women he'd be a part of.

From his great grandfather to his father, all had failed this same task, and now it was up to the son to accomplish it in order to move up the ranks and be seated at the highest table where the One held the third seat for him.

Then the Table of Three would be complete.

He'd slipped a bit back in Oregon and gone too

far in mentioning Hermann's father. The German would need to be handled with more care. These were the right people for the quest, and one in particular was going to be fun to take down and also earn him extra kudos.

Taking a deep breath, Sigurd fought for that needed control now as an excited tremble shook him. Over the past few years he'd had a taste of power as he watched these formidable men and women working for the SineQuaNon, and he wanted to be a part of the society. It was a hunger which consumed him.

This appetite would be assuaged, and if those who got in the way died, so be it. It was part of the cost.

The risk was high. The rewards far greater.

Then democracies and regimes would tumble in the direction *they* dictated. And *they* would stand tall, bringing good fortune to those who understood their wisdom.

Chapter Five

On the long flight to Norway, Hermann alternately sipped champagne and espresso the first class flight cabin attendant brought. He'd worked on charts and research for the first six hours of the journey and was ready to give it a rest.

Abby, in the luxury seat next to him, was busy working her iPad, allowing him plenty of time to think about the irony that was his nature. Stalwart German with the drive to complete to perfection each task, yet born with the deep and passionate emotions that the Germanic people either hid or embraced.

He acknowledged the hardest part to change was his need to focus solely on a task until it was complete. That had been easy when he'd been solo. But bringing in a partner who then had become his lover and now fiancée added a complication he constantly tried to make work. Making decisions using the word "we" versus "me" took some doing.

And for Abby? He knew it was harder for her to think of "we" versus "me." She always leaped before looking. Her fearlessness led her to push beyond any sane boundaries. When he was honest with himself, he hated that she took chances that were, in his opinion, unacceptable. That she didn't see that putting herself at risk was hurting the people around her. He glanced across his seat to her, watching as she continued to work her iPad and absorb all the information she could about Trondheim and Norway. Abby wasn't stupid, she was keenly intelligent, but she was rash. Even before he knew her personally, he had heard of her dramatic adventures.

They'd had many conversations about her risk-taking; their most recent discussion involved her search for the Stone of Heaven. Abby was proud of her ability to cheat death.

He hated it.

She glanced up from her study, then to his closed files and laptop. "Did you figure out the likely scenario of what happened to the plane on its last journey?"

"I did." He signaled the flight attendant for two glasses of champagne. And after they were brought, he touched his glass to hers.

"I've got the basics, but not yet the how. Though I keep thinking sabotage. But by whom and why? Anyway, the plane left the Seefliegerhorst Ilsvika—"

"Translate, please."

"Seaplane base at Ilsvika, which is on the western side of Trondheim, not terribly far from the port where the *Brizo*, my ship, will berth. The plane had to have reached an altitude close to 2000 feet about the time the explosion happened. And since the plane was still in the sight line of the Seenotzentrale—" At her lifted brow, Hermann raised his shoulders quickly in an apologetic shrug. "Sorry, the Search and Recover Coordination Center. The SOS would have been picked up by radio. The plane had to suffer a catastrophic crisis, such as a blown-off tail boom, and it would have gone down fast."

"Good grief, Hermann, you got this from charts?"

"And understanding the plane's mechanics, lift, altitude, etc. In fact, I've bet myself a bottle of Remy Martin Louis XIII cognac that I'm right."

"Then I hope you are. I've never tasted three thousand dollar liquor before."

At that moment, the flight attendants came through first class and made up Abby's seat pod into a bed for sleeping. Abby gave him a sleepy smile, then settled into her freshly laundered down mattress and pulled the light wool blanket over her shoulders.

Hermann watched her face relax as sleep claimed her and wondered again why she couldn't fully accept his gift of love. To be sure, she loved him, but the fact that she was holding back, not fully committing to their life together, bothered him far more than he let on. The last thing he'd do was pressure her into setting a date. Making a lifetime choice. However he also knew he wouldn't be satisfied with the status quo forever.

Not willing to face creating a deadline and losing the only woman he trusted and loved wholly, Hermann turned from her and reopened his computer. He focused intently on the work before him, studying the depth charts of the area where the plane went down.

Scanning the second set of papers, he read the SOS transcript again, memorizing the coordinates. The plane had gone down in a deep, narrow channel before the fjord widened at Trondheim. He believed it was an act of sabotage, but to what gain? If the gold had been deliberately sunk, who would benefit?

Whoever did this had to know the fjord was too deep to dive and thus the gold was not recoverable, at least not in the 1940s. So why was sabotage Hermann's first thought?

Just to keep it out of Nazi hands? That was the only conclusion he could make at the moment, but instinct told him that couldn't be all. The SOS didn't mention anti-aircraft guns. So who brought the plane down? Not the Nazis, of that he was certain. Why plunder it if not to keep it?

The flight attendant brought him another cup of espresso, and as he sipped the hot brew, his thoughts drifted to Sigurd Thorsen. They were going to work together, yet Hermann didn't care for the man. Thankfully Sigurd had booked a different flight. The thought of being cooped up with him, even if it was first class, was too much this soon. *And if you're honest, you have to admit that it takes you a long time to trust. Anyone.*

Hermann saluted himself with his tiny cup and went back to planning the launch site of the AUV and ROV. He would, of course, defer to the captain of his research ship. He looked forward to working with Angus again.

The captain of Hermann's research boat, the *Brizo*, had a varied background. He was as comfortable navigating the judicial system in Scotland as he was the high seas. Hermann rarely got to work with him, usually sending the boat and captain on some task without being aboard.

With a slight smile, Hermann put away the papers and charts and reclined his seat to create his sleep pod. He'd abstained from the down mattress and cover the flight attendants had prepared for Abby and the other travelers. Setting his internal clock for two hours of sleep, he leaned over, lightly kissed Abby on the lips and pulled the blanket back up to her shoulders.

Then he settled back, pushed the button to lift the privacy wall between the seats and concentrated on his breathing, knowing he'd be asleep in five minutes.

Chapter Six

"I wish I could be as chipper as you," Abby groused to Hermann as they deplaned. "I'm betting you slept for less than four hours."

His smile of acknowledgement forced her own lips to curve upward, but still, flying from Seattle to Frankfurt to Norway was a long time to be in a metal tube. Nearly twenty-four hours of flying and transfers to get to Trondheim.

Abby stretched again after exiting the limo Hermann hired to take them from the airport to his ship, docked at the Port of Trondheim.

She studied the *Brizo*, her home for the next few weeks. It was a bigger ship than she'd pictured, probably 150 feet long, painted white and navy. But then again, Hermann never did anything in half measures.

Near the top of the gangplank stood a big man wearing a navy sweater and blue khaki trousers with gold multibar epaulets on his shoulders.

Hermann indicated that she go up first.

"Permission to come aboard, Captain?" she asked before stepping onto the ship.

"Aye, lassie. Welcome to the *Brizo*."

Abby fell instantly in love the Captain Andrews's Scottish brogue. He clasped her hand in his big paw, his skin hardened by his stint on the ocean but whose blue eyes crinkled with the richness of life.

He turned to Hermann and instantly became a bit more formal. "Sir, the ROV is aboard. If you'd like to give the lassie a tour, then we'll meet on the main rear deck."

Hermann clasped Captain Andrews's forearm, in both greeting and agreement. It was obvious to Abby that the men respected and even had a fondness for each other. While there were two decks above the first deck and two below the main deck, Hermann concentrated on the two Abby knew she'd use the most. She could poke around the others later.

Their stateroom, along with those of Captain Andrews and the senior mates, were on the first deck. On the way to the stairs going down, they passed a lab of some sort. Abby wondered just what the *Brizo's* main tasks were when not hunting for treasure.

The main deck housed the galley, mess, lounge area and storage as well various labs and the fantail where Hermann took her to see the Remote Operated Vehicle.

She marveled over the ROV, which looked like a yellow underwater tractor with mechanical, articulated arms and claws. This equipment would do the real work once the wreck was found. A tingle of anticipation ran across her shoulders. She couldn't wait to see what it brought to the surface.

They were interrupted by the captain, who told them that the team from the Norwegian University of Science and Technology was arriving with one of their advanced prototype Autonomous Underwater Vehicles.

"That's stage one. The AUV will use its sonar to find the wreck and won't need to be monitored as the ROV does," Hermann said and left her to continue exploring the ship while he met with the University's crew.

She wandered into the *Brizo's* mess, poured a cup from the large pot and sat at the curved banquette nestled beneath a large window. She let loose a small sigh. So much equipment to make this dive for Viking gold happen, but then the waters of the Trondheim fjord were deep, dark, and bitter cold. Not at all hospitable for human diving, which was one reason the plane hadn't yet been discovered.

Speaking of planes, her job was to check out the real SOS document Sigurd said he'd found. Abby checked her watch; she still had a couple of hours before the Archives closed, so she dialed the number Hermann gave her to call for a taxi.

Finishing her coffee, hoping the caffeine would kick in soon, she headed back onto the dock to find the taxi.

***

The quick trip across the ultra-modern Pirbrua Bridge over the River Nidelva gave her an awesome view of the eclectic mix of the new super-modern structures and the traditional, painted waterfront warehouses that had been turned into houses and shops.

The Regional Archives was housed in a modern building in front of Dora-1, a WWII Nazi submarine bunker. The immensely thick concrete walls of the bunker were an eerie remnant of a regime that shouldn't be forgotten, lest the world repeat its mistakes. Still, it was an odd juxtaposition of historical features and modern structures. Some of the contemporary buildings had even been built on top of the submarine base.

She handed the driver her credit card, wincing a bit at the fare for such a short distance. Then the large mural painted on the outside of the Archives building distracted her, making her smile. Trondheim, and maybe all of Norway, was a fascinating mix of ancient and new.

Signing in at the check-in desk on the first floor, Abby was pleased to learn that Liv, the archivist she'd spoken with on the phone before she left Oregon, was working today.

After the short ride on the sleek elevator to the second floor reading rooms, Abby stopped for a second just inside the door to look around. The modern airy room pulled her forward; this wasn't the usual dark dungeon of records she was used to going through. Shelves after shelves were filled with neat record catalogs.

A petite blonde stood behind the desk. Abby glanced at the name plate on the desk. Indeed it was Liv standing behind it. And she seemed to be staring at something or someone in the glass-walled room adjacent to the records room.

Abby craned her neck to see the profile of a twenty-something handsome man, the only person in the room. A chuckle escaped her and Liv whirled around. Pink stained her cheeks at being caught staring at the hunk.

"He's what we call eye-candy back in the states," Abby said, rubbing her lips to hide her grin.

Liv ducked her head in embarrassment for a moment, but not before stealing another glance at the man.

"Perfect word for him," she said, then coughed as she realized she'd sighed.

This time Abby had to bite her lips to keep from laughing. Giving herself a moment to recover, she stuck out her hand. "I'm Abby Carswell. I called you from Oregon regarding a specific document."

"Liv Trotter," the blonde said, shaking Abby's hand firmly. "Welcome to Trondheim. I have the original pulled for you. You can take it into the reading room," she said, nodding toward the same room that housed the hunk.

"Sure you don't want to take it in there for me?"

"No, I'd probably drop the file, and I think I've had enough embarrassment for one day."

Abby took the folder Liv held out and headed into the room, filled with pale-colored wood desks, lamps and comfortable chairs. She passed the blond, and he glanced up and pinned her for a second with his intense blue-eyed gaze and a quick smile.

No wonder Liv was entranced by the guy.

Abby returned his smile and headed for a table by the window. Settling in, she pulled Sigurd's copy of the plane's SOS document from her bag and gingerly removed the original from the library file. She stared at the document with its multiple strips of paper glued to a Luftwaffe message form. The paper was soft, yet brittle; the glue holding the typed strips was lifting in places, and a corner was bent so badly she was afraid to smooth it out. It felt odd to hold a seventy-plus year-old Nazi death notice.

There was no sense of urgency in the typed words, yet she pictured the men in the plane, the radio operator calling in the SOS as the plane suffered its fate. The pilot doing his best to handle his crippled equipment, most likely knowing he was doomed, as the other members of the crew waited to hit the water. All while the radio operator on the ground was dutifully typing in the distress call, then taking the time to glue the strips on the form before delivering it to the Search and Recovery department.

She wondered just how far the plane had traveled after the distress call. She was sure

Hermann had calculated all that into his plotting for the AUV.

Abby settled down to complete her task, comparing each line of the original message to Sigurd's copy. They were identical.

She'd expected as much. Sigurd would know they'd check. In fact she didn't expect to find any discrepancies in any of what he'd told them.

Glancing at her watch, she realized she'd been gone longer than planned. Time to get moving, report to Hermann that all was good, and then suit up for their test dive. She couldn't wait for that. Even if they weren't going deep or doing anything more than checking out the fjord's sometimes treacherous conditions, she'd still be in an environment that she loved.

Tucking the SOS document back into the folder, she passed behind the man Liv was so gaga over. She glanced down and saw two pictures in a frame he'd set up in front of his stack of documents. Abby leaned in a bit closer to take another look.

"Is that your mother?"

The man looked up, surprised. "Yes."

"You have her eyes. That intense, almost electric, blue. May I?" Abby gestured toward the frame.

At his cautious nod, she picked up the case, its leather feeling old and brittle yet surprisingly heavy. "And the photo in black and white?"

"My grandmother, holding Mom."

She was about to hand it back when she noticed an embossed symbol in the corner. She held it up to the light. *I'll be damned.* "This is an interesting symbol." She pointed to the corner of the frame.

"Celtic I think."

Or Norse.

"Is it a family crest?"

"No idea. You're American, right?"

"Right. Why?"

"No reason, but I'm in need of a cup of coffee, and talking to a fellow yank is always fun. Care to join me?"

"You know, I have an appointment and I'm late. These documents draw you in." She saw agreement in his eyes and thought quickly, not wanting to sever the tie with him if the symbol meant something important. "But I'm coming back in the next day or so to do some more research, so a rain check?"

"Sure. Magnus Jones from Colorado."

"Nice to meet you. See you again. Gotta run."

She hurried out. She didn't want to give her name yet. Maybe the symbol was ubiquitous and she just didn't know it. Or maybe—*What, that it's a symbol for a syndicate? Hold up, Abby girl, now your imagination is working overtime.*

As she returned the original copy of the document to Liv at the help desk, Abby motioned for her to lean in. "You said he's here every day?" she whispered.

Liv nodded. "He said he was taking the summer to do research."

"Lucky you."

Abby left Liv wearing a broad smile while getting the answer she wanted.

***

Abby walked up the gangway of the *Brizo* and waved toward a couple of the crew that were busy on deck. They were helping men she assumed were from the University with what she guessed was the Autonomous Underwater Vehicle. It looked like a long, sleek torpedo and was cradled in a sling on a crane at the side of the boat.

The moment was approaching when they'd actually be hunting for the plane.

Hearing voices as she neared the mess, she made out Hermann's distinct German accent and Sigurd's rhythmic Norse cadence. She'd expected the man to show up any time but still wasn't happy he was here.

It wasn't simply the fact that Sigurd was chauvinistic—there was more to him that bothered her. Maybe it was as Reid discovered, he was simply anxious to right a wrong.

She sucked up her dislike, pasted a smile on her face and walked into the mess. "I think the AUV is being loaded."

Hermann nodded, and she saw the same glow of excitement in his eyes that coursed through her. The hunt was about to begin.

Abby needed to be closer to Hermann than the

fifteen feet that separated them and moved swiftly to stand beside him. If Sigurd hadn't been there, she'd have kissed her man silly. She was so lucky to have someone like Hermann who shared her passion.

"So if I understand this, we use the AUV first, to locate the wreck with its sonar," Abby said. For just a second she wished her trade hadn't become so tech dependent. That it could return to the simpler methods she and Reid had used when they'd started their partnership years ago. The object to search for, along with a map, a bit of payola to grease palms, and leg work to find the treasure. No GPS, satellites, cell phones or Google.

But it wasn't like that now, maybe it never had been that way and she was simply being romantic for the past. She thought about asking Reid sometime, then remembered he was tech fixated as well. He and Hermann were more simpatico that she'd ever thought possible.

The last wreck dive she'd done was a year before the China incident, in warm clear water off Africa, when she was still partnered with Reid. They'd done all the diving and recovery. And while it was deep, it wasn't this deep, and there was light, the opposite of this operation. Which apparently was one reason Hermann wanted to do the dive this afternoon, to "feel" the conditions.

"Yes, the AUV will run supervised but with a preprogrammed grid, using its side and bottom sonar. So when we get pings on the plane, we'll be able to turn on the cameras and get a better look. A supervised mode isn't usual for an AUV, but this isn't the usual search," Hermann said.

"Then once we find the wreck, we'll launch the ROV and direct its movements from the ship. It will search the debris field, pick up and eventually bring up what's found."

"Got it," Abby said and wondered how much detail the sonar images would give them. Guess she'd find out soon enough.

"We should be able to take our first trip out tomorrow morning with the AUV."

"Aye, lassie, you're back," Captain Andrews said with a wink as he entered the galley. He poured a half mug of coffee and drank it in one gulp. "In your honor, the cook is making better brew than usual, which is a good thing or else the crew would be drinkin' it all day and gettin' no work done."

Captain Andrews straightened and turned his attention to Hermann. "Sir, the AUV is stowed. The widened search pattern is being input into the computer."

Abby liked the captain from the moment they'd met. He was no nonsense but had a fabulous sense of humor and an incredible Scottish brogue she could listen to for hours. Hermann told her he'd been a Lord Commissioner of Justiciary in Scotland and, tired of what humans could do to other humans, he turned to the sea, fighting and navigating treacherous waters, including the North

Sea. Little fazed him. He handpicked the permanent crew of twelve from all over the world. None were younger than forty and all had practically lived their lives on the sea.

"Widened search pattern?" Sigurd asked, questioning the captain.

"The plane was still moving when the SOS was sent. So I've increased the search area. The test dive is next." Hermann stood, signaling the briefing was over.

Abby stood with Hermann. "Are you coming on the dive, Sigurd?" *Please say no.*

"Of course. I have my gear on the Zodiac already. But I have a couple of things I must take care of since I've been gone so long. We dive in an hour, right?"

"Right."

"I'll see you then."

Hermann escorted him out as he'd done in Oregon. It wasn't simply courtesy—her cautious German was making sure the man cleared the premises and didn't set any micro devices, such as microphones.

That had happened in Thailand during her first hunt partnered with Hermann, when they searched for the fist-sized emerald known as the Buri Prince. Mined in Brazil, it was sold to a Thai Prince and named for him. Then it was stolen and disappeared for a century.

After discovering for the second time that she and Hermann were not the first to reach a clue,

Hermann swept their hotel room and found the bugs. He left them in place but made sure he and Abby gave out information that sent their competitor on a wild goose chase. That had bought them a forty-eight-hour head start and eventually the prize.

"Did you check the SOS against the original?"

Abby swirled at Hermann's voice, lost in recalling what it had felt like to hold the glowing green gem worth nearly 250 million dollars.

"Sorry, I was remembering Thailand. Yes, the SOS matches exactly. But then something interesting happened. When I was in the reading room of the Archives, I met an American who was researching family ties. I stopped to chat with him for a second and noticed his old and tattered leather picture frame with—get this—the same Celtic symbol embossed in the corner that Sigurd had on his laptop. And you'll never believe his name. Magnus Jones."

As she hoped, Hermann laughed.

"I nearly did the same thing, it's such an unusual name, even sounds contrived, though he doesn't come off that way. Anyway he's there every day, so it might be worthwhile for me to have that coffee with him."

"How did you find out that he was 'there every day'? And having what coffee with him?"

She winked. "I have my sources, and a date with a fellow yank."

"Should I be worried, Liebchen?"

"Never. I keep my sources, my coffee dates and my fiancé separate," she teased.

He pulled her close. "That's excellent," he whispered.

His breath tickled her ear, sending little shivers down her back. Turning her head slightly, her lips aligned with his, and she kissed him with teasing feather kisses at first.

Then the need to be as close as physically possible to this wonderful man swamped her, and she nipped at his bottom lip.

"Abigail," he groaned, pulling her tight against him.

If she could tear off his clothes and take him on the galley bench, she would have. The need to be joined consumed her.

Then Hermann gently lifted his head, breaking their kiss.

She leaned her face against his chest, breathing as hard as he was, his heartbeat thrumming rapidly against her chest. His rhythmic stroking of her hair began to calm them both.

"Did you pick up that Sigurd said he'd been gone for so long? I got the impression he'd been in the states for only a few days."

"Yes. Sigurd Thorsen is more than a student at the University, I believe. But as long as we know our enemy—"

"This is why we're not using a personal sub to go that deep?"

"No reason to."

Abby held his gaze. "Are you playing it uber safe because of me?"

The smile that lit his eyes took her breath away. It was only for her, and she understood the significance. Hermann didn't love easily and rarely trusted anyone enough to get close to them.

"Yes, uber safe, so there's no chance of sabotage this way. It's more than just being safe, Abby. It's going to be cold, deep, and dark down there. Using the ROV makes the most sense. And there is a small window of opportunity to pull this off. The more activity we show around here, the more people are going to show up. Sigurd got the permits, and how he was able to prevent an excavation oversight is curious.

"The dive this afternoon is important, as I said, for the feel of the water, but also because I want to see how Sigurd operates in a team environment. Whether he takes direction well. We'll be using a shot line, and I'm going to have Sigurd go first, then you. I'll bring up the rear."

"Hmmm, sounds like uber safety again."

Hermann shrugged.

Even though the extra protection chafed she said nothing more about being stuck in the middle of two men on their descent. "Okay then. Let me lock the file in the safe and change. See you topside in a couple of minutes." Abby swiftly bussed Hermann on the lips and left the mess.

Their stateroom on the *Brizo* was compact but well appointed, as if she'd expect anything else from Hermann. Teak paneling covered one wall, with a drop-down desk built into it. A stool beneath the desk swiveled up and out to save room. Next to the desk, bookshelves had been fitted with a removable rail that crossed the middle of each shelf to keep the books from falling, and finishing off the wall space was a large cork board.

The other wall, above the double bed, had a bank of windows with roman shades to match the blue bedspread piped in white along with matching pillow shams. The small head, complete with a bathtub, was attached to the cabin

The senior crew had quarters similar to his, and the rest of the crew had berths two decks down. Captain Andrews's larger cabin was across from theirs.

Hermann had designed it all, and it worked efficiently.

Abby lifted the mattress base, which was on pistons, and worked a normal-looking combination safe set into the bed frame. This safe had eight numbers, much harder to crack than those with fewer numbers. After laying the file flat in the watertight chamber on top of the photographs Sigurd had given them, Abby closed and relocked the safe.

She shimmied into the black, lightweight neoprene bodysuit with a yellow stripe from ankle to neck that she'd planned as the underlayer for her cold-water dry suit. Glancing in the full-length mirror on the door, she pirouetted, liking the way the suit clung to her curves.

Abby descended the stairs to Hermann, who was already on the main deck.

"Liebchen, that is an illegal suit, you know," he said, voice rough.

"Indeed."

"Wicked woman."

"Indeed."

***

Zipping over the fjord's waves in the inflatable Zodiac boat loosened one of the knots lodged in Abby's soul since Tori's wedding.

She couldn't wait to get in the water; scuba diving was one of her passions. Another world, inhospitable to humans, yet with its ability to envelope, even cradle her made the sea an ally instead of a foe. Abby needed it as much as the air she breathed on land. It set her free.

And although today's dive wasn't deep for her and Hermann, it exceeded most recreational divers' safety point. Hermann had planned the 180-foot dive vertically down the face of the fjord's massive stone wall to a ledge, with abyss depths just over its edge. The thrill of the unknown beckoned her as would a beacon.

When Hermann told Sigurd of the depth they'd be diving, the man didn't seem bothered in the least, surprising Abby, while Hermann simply raised a brow. However, she knew he'd prepare for the contingency that Sigurd might have a problem, and he'd watch him closely.

She'd checked her own gear before loading it into the Zodiac, knowing that even if the captain or the dive master was excellent, she needed to rely on her own eyes to see that her tanks were filled with the right mixtures, her hoses in great shape and her regulator working.

Captain Andrews anchored the craft, and Abby starting zipping up her dry suit, when Hermann covered her hands with his and finished the job, giving her a quick grin. She then returned the favor and helped him. She left Captain Andrews to help Sigurd work the back shoulder zipper on his suit. The water temps were around a chilly forty degrees, so the complicated and ill-fitting suits were necessary.

Finally in the water, signals and lights checked, Sigurd moved down the shot line first and she followed.

For the first twelve feet the water was brown, caused by the waters of the Nidelva River dumping into the fjord. But as the trio went deeper, the water cleared its murkiness. And as they descended further, sunlight didn't penetrate at all in the fjord. It was like diving in the pitch black. Their facemasks created a narrow beam of visibility that helped negate the sense of claustrophobia.

The red of dead man's fingers delighted her as her light illuminated the eerie, aptly named coral. Fish she'd never seen before darted in and out of their lights, and along the fjord's wall, spiny star fish clung to the rocky face. The experience was other worldly, and her annoyance over Hermann's coddling her on this dive dissolved.

The currents were fierce, just as Hermann had briefed them in the boat. Abby had never seen a shot line move one way with the current and a few feet later, move the exact opposite direction. She could even feel the water's shifting currents on her face where it was unprotected by her facemask.

They reached the ledge above the abyss and Sigurd finned over its surface, inspecting the crevices and corals. Hermann was making notes about the conditions on his dive slate. And the wall with its beautiful and rare creatures beckoned her to inspect it further.

Using Hermann's new flashlight, she was delighted as the concentrated beam cut through the deep gloom along the rough stone face of the wall. Unexpectedly the light revealed a large cluster of red anemones and white corals stuck to the vertical face of the wall like limpets. The transparent polyps of the coral were extended, looking like mini antenna waving erratically, their airy, feathery tentacles reaching out for the food the currents brought.

Below her on the ledge, several spider crabs scuttled over the broken rocks and piles of shells. When she shined her flashlight into a deep crevice, a spider crab poked its bony head out as if to say *Excuse me? This is my world.*

The current pulled at her, and she finned

harder against it to stay close to the wall, but when she looked down, the ledge was gone, only inky darkness loomed below. Despite her intense leg work, the currents had moved her from the ledge.

Abby fought her panic, knowing good divers died when terror overtook them. Clinging to the wall, she finally summoned the courage to let go with one hand. She played her flashlight up and down using the motion as a signal beacon, but instantly realized that if she could barely see the tiny pricks of light indicating Hermann and Sigurd's position, they'd have a hard time seeing hers. She'd moved out of range.

A swish of current tore at her, and before she could grip the rock of the wall with both hands, she was pushed downward into the abyss below.

Wildly playing her light around she spied a small ledge and finned toward it with all her might, bucking the current, her muscles quivering from the strain, knowing reaching it would give her a minute to recover if she could make it to a firm standing point and hold on.

Landing on the narrow outcropping kicked up a huge bloom of silt and instantly Abby was enveloped. She fumbled for handholds on the wall, and finally found purchase. She could barely see her gauges but knew from instinct her bottom time was nearly done and she'd need to head up and start decompression. Worse, she was breathing faster and depleting her tanks too quickly.

Regrettably, heading up meant releasing her

grip on the wall, which also meant letting the current have her again. She didn't think she had the legs to fin upward.

She was frozen. She had no idea what to do next. She'd never experienced this kind of fear in the water that she so loved.

Think girl. It's up to you to survive. Help isn't coming.

Pinning one fin against a rock and hooking her arm around a small outcrop of coral, she played her light, thankful the plume of silt was lightening as the current swept it away. Three short, three long, three short. Her own SOS in the fjord. Damned ironic.

Her gauge showed her she was over time. It was swim up or die.

Kicking hard, knowing it was her only chance, Abby looked straight upward at her goal. She pushed from her mind the deadly consequences of rising without her decompression stops.

Until something snagged her fin and pulled her down.

Abby kicked against it, realizing a second later Hermann was beside her. She blinked as his face mask lights shone directly into her face.

She pointed to her gauge showing her tanks nearly empty and pointed to his, shaking her head no.

He held her head still, then pointed to his auxiliary and trimix tank and gave her the universal okay sign.

Pointing to himself, asking her to trust him, he held on to her as they descended, giving her the proper decompression time. They shared his regulator as the minutes ticked by, then rose to the next stage.

When they had one more decompression stop, Hermann deployed his emergency yellow buoy to mark their point of surface.

Chapter Seven

Thankfully Captain Andrews had binoculars up, and the Zodiac got to them quickly. Abby trembled with exhaustion, and Hermann kept her afloat, one arm on the buoy and the other around her.

Sigurd was beside himself, practically falling out of the boat to help them aboard.

"Do we need the hyperbaric chamber, sir?" Andrews asked as he piloted the craft swiftly over the fjord.

"No, I don't believe so," Hermann said. "I think I got her down in time. Thank you both for your help."

Abby thought his answer oddly stiff but added her nodded thanks.

She was too drained to attempt to take off her dry suit and leaned back against the large inflatable pontoons of the boat. The sea had never treated her so badly.

History repeated itself. China, and Hermann had almost died. The Yucatan and she had almost died, and now Norway and again she'd nearly shed her mortal bonds. Was this curiosity, this need for the adrenaline rush above all else, finally going to claim her or Hermann?

Visions of Tori's serene face as she walked down the petal strewn aisle on Alfred's arm, and Reid's pride beaming back played in Abby's mind. Why couldn't she do this? Settle down, be a wife to the man she loved. Share the rest of their lives together bonded by marriage?

I wish I understood why.

Forcing away those images and the question she couldn't answer, she turned her head and looked again at Hermann, seeing immense sorrow on his face.

Her soul stilled. Fear and anger she would understand, but this? This looked like he was giving up on her.

Reaching out, she grasped his hand, half expecting him to avoid contact.

His fingers curled around hers, but loosely.

She squeezed tighter. Abby needed him to be her courtly Hermann, to bring her fingers to his lips as he'd done countless times before.

Instead his touch felt perfunctory, even sterile, as if he'd just saved a stranger. Hermann was building a wall between them.

Bile rose in her throat, and she needed to get off the Zodiac or lose what little was in her stomach.

Andrews made quick work of reaching the *Brizo*, and Hermann closely followed her up the ladder from the smaller boat as her legs visibly trembled.

He got her into their cabin and out of her dry suit. She felt like a child, leaning against him as he pulled off her gear, then her body suit down to her undies.

"Abigail, you need rest. I'll check on you for any signs of the bends, but I think you'll be fine. And remember, Tori and Reid will be here later this evening, and I'm sure you'll want to catch up with them both."

Hermann gently thumbed across her jaw, then left without a kiss. She'd wanted to turn and kiss his hand, but his use of her full name in a monotone stopped her as did the formality of his words.

A tear slid down her cheek, and she didn't bother wiping it away.

Had this been an accident or had she just decided to take a risk and not follow Hermann's instructions to stay close because he'd swaddled her in cotton, putting her between himself and Sigurd on the shot line?

Abby stared at the ceiling, unable to answer.

Chapter Eight

"Liebchen, you look well. The flight wasn't that bad, eh?"

Tori held her arms out to hug Hermann, only to be enveloped by his intense bear hug. "Actually it wasn't bad when I was asleep," she said, smiling.

Hermann released her and shook Reid's hand.

Tori couldn't believe Abby wasn't there waiting for them as well and had to wait a few more minutes before her twin entered the *Brizo's* mess.

She practically flew into Tori's arms, and her hug was as intense as Hermann's. Both embraces felt on the edge of tense, Abby's more so. And she looked drained to the point of exhaustion.

The bond between twins was always strong; however, Tori and Abby's bond was electrical. It had waned until last year, but grew stronger after the crisis in the Yucatan, and now Tori felt a shadow between her sister and Hermann.

What had happened in a mere five days since the wedding?

Hermann had a sadness deep in his eyes and while polite, even jovial, tension hung like a cloud between them. He barely touched Abby, nor were they sharing those knowing glances that lovers do.

A lover's quarrel? Abby and Hermann usually didn't let those last long, each strong enough in character to demand the air be cleared. And from what Abby had told her, it always was. Not this time, apparently.

They all sat at the U-shaped table in the mess, on a built-in banquette covered in sturdy vinyl that followed the table's curve. Tori had drained her first cup of coffee and needed another if she was going to concentrate on the report her husband was giving on the medallion.

She'd heard bits and pieces when he ah-ha'd as he'd found information, but hadn't heard the whole history. She got up to fill a carafe with coffee from the large urn.

Just then a sizable man entered the mess. He blinked as he looked from her to Abby and back to her until his face creased with a wide grin. “Lassie, welcome aboard,” he boomed and clasped her hand in both of his.

Hermann made the introductions, and Tori instinctively trusted the captain.

He was a bit more circumspect and reserved with his greeting to Reid, yet admiration glinted in the captain's eyes. Obviously Hermann had filled the captain in on her husband, and she still marveled that Reid and Hermann were now on such good terms.

Captain Andrews touched his finger to his

brow and left them.

Tori brought the carafe back to the table and filled their cups.

"When do we get to meet this Sigurd Thorsen" Reid asked. "Is he staying on the ship?"

"Not at the moment," Hermann said. "You'll get your chance to meet him tomorrow, or the next day at the latest."

Tori settled next to her husband and watched with humor as he drained half his cup of the black brew, then began his report.

"So it appears the shape at its heart is a trinity knot, which is very common even today," Reid said. "But this one is interwoven three times with three points that look almost like trefoils. I'm guessing the points are important. Since your guy Sigurd is Norse, and we're looking for Viking gold, I looked for threes in Viking mythology. Odin's traditional three is interlocked triangles. Then I looked up the trinity knot, which is usually considered to be a trinity to love, honor, and protect, but that didn't fit either." He paused to take another gulp of coffee.

Tori turned to Abby when Reid mentioned the traditional trinity and saw her wince and look at Hermann with stark pain in her eyes. Tori peeked at Hermann and noted his eyes weren't laser-focused as normal.

Catching Reid's glance, she lifted her shoulders in the slightest of shrugs and saw a wicked gleam in her husband's eyes.

"So then George and his chimps saved the

queen and all was well," he said.

Tori just stared at her husband and started laughing. She couldn't help it, and put her full cup on the table before she spilled it all over the floor.

"What? George?" Hermann said, completely confused.

"Gotcha. Did you hear a word of what I was saying?"

"Triangles," Abby said.

"Sorry, Reid, I lost you after trinity," Hermann said, minus his usual blue-eyed twinkle.

"That's okay, I was getting long-winded anyway. I found another trinity of sorts and this seems to fit better. Odin's three residences in Asgard. Gladsheim which was like a council chamber, Valaskjálf which was built from solid silver and Valhalla which was lined with gold." He lifted his shoulders in a shrug. "That's all I have. I can't find that specific shape."

"I saw the symbol again on a frame. An American doing research in the Archives, and it was embossed on an old leather frame." Abby said. "So maybe it's more common than we thought."

"Then I should have found it," Reid said.

"And remember, Sigurd did not want you to see it, Abby. He was unquestionably irritated at the prospect that you had."

"If this symbol concerns you, then I say go with your gut. Instead of annoying Sigurd again, I think we should have a second meeting with the owner of the frame," Reid suggested. "See if we can gather any more information on why he also has the image. Maybe it's some sort of family crest, even though I couldn't find it."

Tori knew that if Reid couldn't find it, the information had to be buried deep and that her husband would be annoyed enough to dig until he found more.

"Then I'll go back tomorrow," Abby volunteered quickly. Too quickly.

"Remember, the AUV goes out tomorrow. We're taking the *Brizo* near the SOS coordinates to launch it, saving time, we hope," Hermann said.

Tori thought it odd that Abby didn't want to be on hand for the launch. She was definitely avoiding Hermann.

But Tori couldn't help her this time. She wasn't sure she could endure being on a boat without having a bit of down time after all those hours in the air. She looked at Reid, hoping he got the message in her gaze. Tori didn't want to wimp out, but water still haunted her as did air travel. Their parents had died in an airplane crash over the Atlantic while coming home as a surprise for their daughters' thirteenth birthday. That day everything had changed between the girls.

"Hey, you guys do the boat stuff, Tori and I will do the land stuff and meet the guy " Reid said easily, making it a simple statement, but just the right touch of brooking-no-argument.

Abby opened her mouth. "But I think I'd—"

"Ja, that makes sense," Hermann interrupted.

"I don't think Tori is quite ready to be on the sea."

Abby shut her mouth and sent her an apologetic look, then quickly filled them in on her meeting with Magnus Jones, Liv, her Archives contact and the leather frame with the pictures. There was nothing more to be said.

The silence was awkward. "Hey, guys, I'm beat. Tomorrow is already here, so we're going to head off," Tori said, forcing a yawn.

She hugged Hermann and Abby goodbye, and they left the boat, refusing Hermann's escort back to the hotel.

After walking down the *Brizo's* gangway, Reid grabbed her hand and held on tightly. "Even though it's a bit chilly, I need a walk—up for that?"

"Yes. I don't think I could stand to be in the hotel after being so long in the jet. First class and all, it was still a metal tube. Did you get the vibes—" Tori stopped, feeling guilty talking about her sister.

"Yes."

And he squeezed her hand. All her guilt fled. She could talk to Reid about anything. What an incredible gift. "I'd hoped it was just me being overly jet-lagged."

"Unfortunately, no. It felt pretty strained."

"Yeah. Not just a lover's spat. I wonder what happened?"

Reid tucked her arm in his, another one of his Southern gentleman habits she quite adored. Even though it was now past twelve o'clock, the midnight sun hung on the horizon. Twilight was hours long this time of year so they could easily see the pathway as they walked along the length of the outer pier to the breakwater and its lighthouse.

A light wind whipped the waves against the stones of the barrier. The night was cool and the humidity made the temperature drop another few degrees. *Definitely not Hawaii warm.* A shiver shook her. Reid instantly wrapped his arms around her and brought her close against his chest.

"See the little island out there?" Reid said, pointing to what looked like a fortress in the middle of the fjord. "That's Munkholmen. It has a gruesome history from King Olav on, but now it's a great spot for a day trip."

Tori knew he was trying to take her mind off Abby and Hermann and loved him all the more for it. "It looks like a short boat trip. Maybe if we have time, we'll try it."

He tipped up her chin and captured her lips in a possessive kiss. "Only if you're up for it, Darlin'."

Tori turned in his arms to look at the *Brizo* across the inlet, moored to the shore-side pier. On the *Brizo*, a few hands were securing the boat for the night. She could see a silhouette against what she supposed was one of the cabins. A deep sigh escaped her. "I hope they work it out."

"Me too. They're both headstrong and stubborn. Makes for a hard mix."

"And you?" Tori teased. "You're pretty headstrong yourself, even stubborn."

“Ah, but you've tamed me.”

“Not in a million years.” That earned her a deep rumble of laughter.

“I think our hotel room is calling.”

“My jet lag is fleeing as we talk.”

Their leisurely stroll turned into a speed-walking session back to the hotel a block from the pier.

***

Tori and Reid had left the *Brizo*. As happy as she was to see her twin, Abby was exhausted, not only from the dive but from the strain between her and Hermann. She was pulling her suitcase from the small closet when she felt a frisson of electricity spark between them. It invariably happened when Hermann was near—corny, but so true.

He closed the door softly.

“I think I should get a room at the hotel,” Abby said, choking back tears as she kept her back to the door. “We can come up with some excuse.”

“I think that's a mistake.”

Abby whirled from the compact closet. “I thought you'd be happy if I put some distance between us. I don't understand why you seem—”

“Abigail, we must talk this through, but this isn't the right moment, as I'm sure you'll agree. Nor is it fair to burden Tori and Reid with our personal issue, especially since it's still their honeymoon. I love you, you are part of my heart, but I cannot watch you try, once again, to destroy yourself. At the end of this hunt we talk, and if we can't find a reason for your behavior—"

"For God's sake, Hermann, it was an accident. I wasn't on a suicide mission. My 'behavior' as you call it—"

He held up a hand. "I retract that word. Can we behave normally for the time we're here?"

Abby shot him a questioning look even as her heart constricted to half its size. "Can you?"

"Ja. For the sake of Tori and Reid, I can do this. Then afterward, we talk."

"I don't think I want a ticking bomb between us the whole time we're here."

"Think back on my words, and you'll realize it's only a ticking bomb if you want it to be. I know you're exhausted. Go to sleep, rest for tomorrow, and I'll be quiet when I return from the last plotting session with Andrews."

Hermann proved his words as he brushed her forehead with his lips, then left.

Stripping to the scrap of lace she wore as panties, Abby pulled on a T-shirt of Hermann's but only felt more miserable as she crawled between the cold sheets, where his clean, slightly woodsy scent surrounded her.

Yanking off the shirt, she threw it against the wall and waited for the relief to come. When it didn't, she got up and folded the shirt neatly on the foot of the bed so she could slip it on in case of a boat emergency. With an entirely male crew, leaving the cabin wearing nothing but undies that barely covered anything wasn't wise.

Abby left the light on over Hermann's side of the bed. She *was* exhausted and needed to turn off her brain and her heart. But it just didn't happen.

Hearing footsteps, she glanced at the clock on the built-in bedside table and saw that an hour had passed, but sleep remained elusive. Closing her eyes, she forced her breathing to be slow and rhythmic.

"Liebchen, you can't fool me," Hermann said softly as he closed the door. She heard the zipper of his trousers, the soft movement of the hanger as he put his clothes away, a habit of his, no matter how tired he was. As he climbed into bed, Abby felt the mattress sag and the sheets pull across her as he rolled onto his side, but no breath on her face. He was turned away from her.

Through it all, she kept her eyes closed. It was going to be hell if she didn't figure out some way to "act normal" for the rest of their sojourn in Norway.

Or, as Hermann said, figure out why she seemed to flirt with death—the same reason that caused her inability to speak those two important words, I do.

***

It was early morning but Tori couldn't sleep in. She'd only been asleep for a few hours and now stood at the hotel's window admiring the new day. The sun glinted off the harbor of Trondheim and bold Norwegian coffee wafted its scent from the mugs Reid held.

Not Hawaii, but pretty darn wonderful. And who'd have thought she'd be a world traveler when just a year ago, Tori would have done anything to avoid leaving her train for any reason.

“I've got to take a shower and wash the travel off me,” she said between sips of the hot brew.

Reid followed her into the stark modern bathroom and settled against the counter as she turned on the shower's taps, stripped and stepped into the steaming stream of hot water.

“Are you comfortable with the plan to check out this guy while pretending to be Abby?” Reid asked. “After all, we didn’t get much of a chance to hash out the details after we got back to the room. We were pretty, um—”

“The word you're looking for is sated. Completely and utterly sated. And yes, I think it'll work. And I know you’ll have it all worked out before we actually get there. Hand me my mug, pretty please?”

Tori heard his chuckle as he placed the mug in her outstretched, dripping hand. Moving to one corner of the tiled cubicle so the shower of water didn't dilute the brew, she took a gulp, then handed the mug back to him.

“Doesn't the soap get into it?” he teased.

“Of course not—I wouldn't ruin a fabulous cup of coffee.”

Regretfully turning off the taps, she stepped out of the shower into the warm towel Reid held open for her.

“Simply not fair. It's our honeymoon, and we're on a bloody schedule,” he complained.

Tori wrapped the warmth around her, tucked in the ends sarong-style, and kissed the pouting lips of her husband. “But gold awaits.”

He laughed, picked her up and twirled around. “Yes it does, so hurry up.”

***

A taxi dropped Tori and Reid on the northeast side of the hulking mass of the Dora-1 submarine bunker, away from any windows of the Trondheim Archives. Thankfully Reid had quickly worked his Internet magic and found exactly the layout of the archives and where to hide from stray glances. It wouldn't do for this Magnus Jones guy to see them together. Not yet.

“Be safe, Darlin'. I don't think this guy sounds dangerous, but I'll be there—use our signal if you feel anything is off.”

Snatching a quick kiss, he saluted her and headed across the parking lot and into the Archives. While she waited the five minutes they'd decided on, Tori mused again at the way Reid barreled into her life and pulled her from her shell, giving her his love, being her best friend.

Glancing at her watch, she realized she'd run over the five-minute mark they'd set for her to follow. She hustled to the Archives.

Approaching the help desk on the second floor, Tori worried for a moment when she didn't see Reid or the man Abby had described as Magnus until she looked into the adjacent, light-filled reading room. Quite the opposite of that gray bulk of wartime history just outside the archives.

She learned from the man at the desk that Liv wasn't there today, so that was one less scene to play in this game of charades.

Inside the reading room, Reid had his tablet propped up in front of him and, beside it on the table, an archives catalog he must have grabbed from the stacks outside. Magnus Jones had a huge pile of documents in front of him, and she thought she saw the little leather frame propped up, peeking from behind the mound of paper.

Show time.

Tori had pulled her hair back into the style Abby had worn yesterday and was confident that she could pull off the pretense of being her sister. Even Reid at their first encounter hadn't known right away that she wasn't Abby, and he'd been her twin's partner for years. Only Alfred had been able to instantly tell one twin from the other.

Now Tori could add Reid and Hermann to the short list of those who knew the subtle differences between her and her twin.

Tori took a deep breath and headed for Magnus. She stopped and stood at the desk in front of him.

"Hey, Magnus, sorry I had to rush off yesterday. I was late as it was for my appointment. Do you have time for that coffee now?"

He looked up and grinned. "That sounds really

good. It's been a bust this morning, until now. I didn't catch your name the other day."

"Sorry, as I said, I was in a rush. Victoria Carswell from Oregon," she said, remembering Abby had said that was the way Magnus had introduced himself.

Tori noticed he carefully slipped the leather frame into the pocket of his light-weight nylon jacket, then packed up his laptop. They left the room, and he turned in his files, got his receipt and told the man he'd be back in a bit for them. The archivist put them aside with a nod; he must be used to working with people who came and went.

With an effort, Tori refrained from looking at Reid as they headed out of the reading room to the café upstairs.

There weren't many people in the café as it was early for lunch. She and Magnus had their choice of tables, which carried on the theme of blond wood and modern design the rest of the building embraced.

Tori was hungry and looked over the fresh salad bar, deciding instead on a sandwich of paper-thin fish topped with cucumbers and other veggies. Coffee seemed to be the beverage of choice as the few people in the café had white porcelain cups of the brew in front of them. No wasteful paper cups in this café.

As they reached the register, Magnus refused her offer to pay. Tori led the way to a table near the bank of windows, and sat facing the entry.

From the corner of her eye, she saw Reid enter the cafe, grab a coffee, and choose a table close by. He sat facing her direction but didn't glance at her once. He got comfortable and worked his tablet.

Magnus silently sipped his coffee. After taking a bite of her sandwich, Tori searched for a way to break the ice. "So, you have a huge pile of documents—what are you working on?"

"My heritage. I have no idea where our family came from and why I have this . . . odd name."

"It is a bit . . . different."

"It's downright ridiculous. As a kid I used to hate it. The nicknames were awful, like Magwuss."

"Seriously? That's mean. But I had one too, The Queen, because of Queen Victoria. I hated it. I was taller than everyone else...anyway, I interrupted you." Tori waved her hand imperiously for him to continue, earning the laugh she'd hoped to get from Magnus.

"I complained to Mom, threatening to change it. Each time she patiently told me that I was given the name as a way to honor my great grandfather's name. And then when I grew older and still hated the name, I'd press her about great grandfather's family. Her reply was always the same, that she knew little of our family, only that we were second-generation immigrants. She always immediately dropped the subject, so I'm guessing it was a sore spot with her.

"But before she died, she finally admitted that her mother had once mentioned a Norway connection, all gone now, but those were her roots."

"Oh, I'm sorry. When did she die?"

"Christmas." The pain of his recent loss still raw in his voice, he continued. "So I took the summer off and here I am, seeing if there are any roots."

"You must miss her terribly."

"I do."

They sat for a moment in silence, drinking their coffees, black as Hades and wonderfully strong.

"I hope you don't mind, but that symbol, the one embossed inside the frame—I looked it up last night. It's Celtic in origin." Damn, stretching the truth came too easily in this business.

"Why would you bother?" he asked, a frown forming.

She lifted her palms upward. "I love symbols. I'm a jeweler and symbols are a great way to tell a story. It's often the interaction between art and myth, and when you add gemstones, that adds another dimension to the story. It's fun.

"The Vikings had a lot of symbols and a lot of myths. They borrowed from the Celts and other cultures—that's one reason I'm here. I want to design some new jewelry and, you know, Vikings are hot right now."

Apparently her story worked, because his slight frown vanished. "Well, I don't think my symbol is important, but it's another clue I guess I can chase down."

"You really have nothing more?"

"I'm getting nowhere with the name Magnus. It's a common name here. Before I left the states I did follow up my grandmother, Brigitte Jones. Her maiden name was Hammersfeld on the marriage license, but I can't find anything before that or about her birth or her parents. I did find a Hammersfeld in Iceland, but they had no offspring on the census records."

"Brigitte must be a fairly common name here as well." Tori ate the last bit of her sandwich, then took a sip of her coffee as she studied Magnus over the cup's rim. He sounded totally legit to her.

"The Internet is a great thing, unless you're trying to stay hidden. Brigitte married my grandfather in Greenland. And I found out Grandfather Jones was an American engineer. So I worked backwards, and those Hammersfelds did emigrate to Greenland, and their documents show they had a daughter, Brigitte."

"It sounds like quite the mystery. Maybe she was adopted?" Tori put down her cup, then glanced at Reid across the room. He didn't look up from his tablet, but she knew he saw her. She wiped her hands on the napkin and clasped them on the table, their signal for time to go.

Her phone buzzed just then. She made a big deal out of checking the message, knowing already it said "meet you outside."

"Oh, good news, there is a man who has some

Baltic Amber for sale. I have to dash."

She rose and extended her hand to Magnus. "I hope we get to meet again, and I hope you have better luck finding your roots. Thanks for the coffee and sandwich."

"My pleasure. Are you going to be here long?"

"Maybe another few days," she hedged.

He scribbled quickly on his napkin. "Here's my email—"

"Great. I'll send you one, then you'll have mine."

Carefully tucking the napkin on which he'd scrawled his email into her purse, she waved goodbye and rushed out.

She left the café, took the stairs down three flights, and once out of the Archives, headed back to their prior rendezvous point at the Dora-1 bunker.

The sheer magnitude and hulk of the gray concrete structure gave her goose bumps. When planning their rendezvous point, Reid had brought up satellite pictures of it, showing the new modern construction on top of the bunker and the five submarine bays that still had water in them. The concrete sides were nearly ten feet thick and the roof over eleven feet. Built to withstand repeated aerial assaults.

"So?"

Tori spun around. She was so absorbed in the awful history of the building in front of her, she hadn't heard Reid approach.

"It was interesting. Have you heard from Hermann and Abby?"

"Yes, the *Brizo* will be back within the hour. The launch of the AUV was successful."

"Then when we meet up, I'll tell you the story and we can decide if Magnus is worth following.

Chapter Nine

Half listening to Tori, Abby fought her stomach cramps as she glanced around the deck bar on the ninth floor of the Clarion Congress. Hermann had done well to pick this hotel for the newlyweds. The location was perfect, a mere stroll from the pier and the *Brizo*. The style was sophisticated modern and this deck was impressive, its view of the fjord unparalleled. The marina directly below was, at the moment, busy with a cruise ship that had just docked.

This was exactly the place she would have picked for a rendezvous with Hermann. They'd sip champagne and nibble on herring, cozy in one of the deep chairs that accommodated two, and the world around them would recede. They had a knack for being alone in a crowd.

But perhaps that was never to happen again if Hermann really was going to give up on her.

Putting a hand to her stomach, the wave of cramps passed. A physical symptom that had begun yesterday with Hermann's bombshell of an announcement.

You knew this could happen.

But I didn't really think he could give me up so easily.

Easy? Cripes, it's not easy—didn't you see the agony on his face when he told you? At least be honest with yourself.

Abby focused back on their group just as Tori finished her story.

Hermann swigged the last of his beer and put the bottle on the table. "So, it seems a strange coincidence that two people we've met would have the same symbol. One who seemed to be concerned we saw it and the other less than concerned. Both men are in Trondheim, both about the same age. I don't believe much in coincidences, but then, stranger synchronicities have happened and have been just that."

"Magnus seemed very sincere and open, but then I don't have your," Tori swept her arm wide to include all of them, "background in reading people."

"Wrong. Didn't Alfred say you could see a puzzle better than most? Even me?" Abby pretended to pout.

"A puzzle is one thing, evaluating people another."

"No, Tori, it's not. You have instincts I trust," Hermann said with a gentle smile.

The kind of smile that always made Abby melt. She watched it have the same effect on Tori, and Abby's gut burned again.

Reid pulled out his cell phone and pushed a few buttons. "I've got a search going on Magnus, and so far nothing is suspect in his background. He's led a fairly clean life. Got busted by his high school for smoking pot and did a two-day suspension. Worked a ton of odd jobs from janitor to dive instructor to bartender. His mother, Cindy Jones, got divorced before Magnus was born, and reverted back to her maiden name. They lived simply. At times, Cindy worked several jobs. So it must have been tight for them. He's a PhD candidate in mechanical engineering at the University of Colorado."

Hermann smiled just a bit. The kind of ah-ha smile that made Abby wonder just what he was going to do with that information.

"I'm not getting any pings on Brigitte Hammersfeld's life as a child in Iceland prior to moving to Greenland," Reid continued. "She became a naturalized American citizen when she and her husband, returned to the States. And there seems to be no connection or communication between Magnus and Sigurd," Reid said.

"How do you know that?" Tori asked, pride shining in her gaze.

Abby understood that pride. Reid Hunter had inherited his grandmother's knack and love of finding the impossible, and his reputation, while not as public as Abby's, was well known in the circles that mattered. And before he'd fallen head over heels for Tori, Reid had been either flush or broke, usually smiling in either condition. Then China, and all had changed. But now life had moved back to level for all of them.

"Pure genius, of course," Reid said with a grin. "No, it's about knowing where and how to mine the data. There are sources the authorities just don't want you to know you can access, and you have to cover your tracks. Sometimes it takes good ol' palm greasing. And other times it just takes a smile, like in Merida, remember?" he said with a wink.

Abby watched with sad amusement as Tori's cheeks flushed. What was that about? Time for some more girl talk.

No! Bad idea. If they talked, she'd have to explain what was going on with Hermann.

"I think we should continue on with the charade—"

"It's a very good one. You could make a mint off it by using each other as alibis for your little con artist ring."

Abby looked up, stunned to see Magnus, drink in hand, standing behind Reid's chair.

"I've seen all three of you, except this gentleman here," he said, tilting his drink in Hermann's direction.

Reid jumped up, facing Magnus, while Hermann rose languidly, offering him his hand. "Hermann Weiss, Weiss Engineering. We don't con or steal, we find. Have a seat, Mr. Jones."

Magnus's eyes widened so quickly when he heard Hermann's name and company, Abby almost laughed. She wondered if he realized he practically licked his lips at meeting one of the world's best engineers. Quickly pulling himself together, he gazed at each of them, as if sizing them up, then dragged forward a chair.

Only then did Reid sit.

"Abigail Carswell," she introduced herself. "I met you first. You've had coffee with my twin, Tori."

"Reid Hunter, Tori's husband," Reid introduced himself and held out a hand.

Now they were a *cozy* fivesome.

"Why the need for all the games?" Magnus asked, politely but with an edge that didn't surprise her.

***

"Not games, Mr. Jones. The need for certainty," Hermann said. Now that they'd been discovered, there was little need for anything other than the truth. Not the whole truth, of course, just enough to satisfy.

"Abby and I, and Reid and Tori, have a penchant, shall I say, for finding lost things. Some of those things were only hearsay, but we've found some of those as well."

"And your quest this time?"

"You're here on a quest as well, I understand." Hermann sidestepped the question for the moment, giving Magnus an opening to talk about himself. Most people loved to talk about themselves.

"I am. And your quest?"

This man wasn't one of them. Hermann made a quick decision and moved a few steps to the hotel deck's railing. "See the research ship docked there?" He pointed. "It's the *Brizo*. My ship. We have an AUV search going on at the moment. And when it finds the wreck, we'll send down an ROV."

"Why the need for a charade? You have to have permits for this. People know."

Abby nodded. "Yes, they do, and it's not the wreck we're worried that you know about. It's the medallion on your picture frame. We've seen the same medallion, and it may be connected to this hunt. So we wanted to know more about you."

Magnus looked right at Tori. "You gave a great story. I bought it about you being a jeweler."

"But I am one. And what I said was true, mostly."

"How'd you know I'd be there that day?"

"Liv told me—" Abby broke off as she didn't see a flicker of recognition in Magnus's eyes. "Liv from the archives? The one who can't keep her eyes off you?"

Magnus actually blushed as he nodded.

"She told me you'd been there daily. I pretty much pulled it out of her, so don't be mad at her."

"My search, as I told *you*," Magnus looked at Tori, "is to find my past. My heritage. I have few leads and limited resources, so the only way for me to do this is to go through as much of the archives as I can, focusing on personal records. It's slow and painstaking."

"Census records?" Abby asked.

"I've been working on them and found an interesting complication. A census was taken in 1930, but not another until 1946, because of the war. I've gone backwards on ages, and if Brigitte was born here, she'd fall into that range. But I don't know that she was born here. It's pure speculation."

"Have you gone to churches to look in their registries?" Tori asked.

"I'm starting on that next week. But which one? Twenty-one major churches are listed in Trondheim. Listen, I've spent money I could ill afford and consulted several top genealogical experts, and they've given me a list to follow, so I think I'm covered on what I should be doing—"

A waitress came over, flouncing her short skirt right at Magnus's eye level, and winking at him before she turned to her attention to Hermann.

"Would you like another round?"

Hermann nodded to her, watching Magnus from the corner of his eye, seeing him blush again at the waitress' actions. He seemed too naive to be a part of a conspiracy.

"And, Mr. Jones, what are you drinking?"

"Vodka with a twist."

Good, he was going to stay a bit longer. Abby smiled.

"So what is so important about this wreck? And how old is it?" Magnus asked after the waitress winked at him again and left.

All eyes turned to Hermann. Good also, because he'd decided to be somewhat candid.

“1940s.”

“Nazi?”

“Ja. It's possible it contains plundered art that belongs to the people of Norway.”

“Seriously? You're doing a ‘Monuments Men’ type of operation?”

“Yes.”

“Anything in the fjord that long would be ruined.”

“More than paintings were stolen by the Wehrmacht.”

“Ah. Going to tell me what's down there?”

“No. I'm afraid not.”

Magnus grinned, and he looked younger, less stressed.

“If I had the time, I guess I'd try and find out, but I used all my savings to come here for the summer, and I need to focus on my own task.”

“You're a grad student in engineering, aren't you?” Reid asked.

Hermann got the look Reid casually sent him. Magnus knew Weiss Engineering, so he'd know more about Hermann than about the rest of them.

Hermann dipped his head, acknowledging Reid's warning.

“Yes, I want to teach at university level and for that, a PhD is pretty much necessary. My prof wasn't teaching this summer, so there weren't classes available for me to do my teacher's assistant gig. So as I said, I used most of my savings to get here. I was going to rent an apartment, but I got a job—"

"Here you are, Magnus," the waitress said, bringing their order and giving their guest his before serving them. Hermann was intrigued that she knew Magnus's name. For a poor grad student, this was a fairly expensive haunt. Was he a regular?

"Thanks, Marta. As I was going to say, I got a job bartending at this hotel in the evenings in exchange for some pocket change and a room. Not what you expected, I'm sure," he finished with a wide smile.

***

"I thought I'd find you all here. Your Captain Andrews is a mule when it comes to telling me anything about your whereabouts," Sigurd said loudly, standing not more than six feet away.

Abby blinked. Well, how much more odd could this gathering become?

"Are these our additional team members?"

Reid got up and introduced Tori and himself.

"Ah, it was your wedding I crashed," Sigurd said. He smiled, but it didn't quite reach his eyes.

"Join us and meet our friend, Magnus Jones," Reid offered.

Abby saw the quick look he shot to Magnus that said "follow our lead." Meaning Reid instinctively trusted him.

Sigurd pulled up one of the deep, cushioned

chairs, settling in. “I wasn't aware you were with a friend. Sorry to intrude. Do you live here, Mr. Jones?”

“Magnus, please. And no, just for the summer, doing a bit—”

“Ha, not a *bit* of anything—Magnus is doing research for his engineering PhD. I'd met him awhile back.”

Abby loved Reid's play on meaning. He wasn’t lying, he had met him awhile back, Sigurd didn't need to know that awhile was only a few minutes ago.

“Right,” Magnus glanced quickly again at Reid, who smiled. “And since I saw Mr. Weiss here, I wanted to pick his brain about a question—”

“On vacation, I reminded you,” Hermann interrupted Magnus with an easy laugh.

“Yeah, yeah, I know, but I also know you can't resist talking about your latest invention. Listen, I gotta go, got a conference downstairs, and they are a thirsty bunch. See you around, eh?”

Magnus gulped his drink and headed off with a wave.

“Magnus works here to help with his expenses. You know how expensive Trondheim is,” Abby inserted smoothly, earning a look of admiration from Hermann.

She felt the tingle of pleasure in his approval, then remembered that he was “acting” normal.

Forcing her lips into a slight smile, Abby hoped she too could play-act.

"Any other people you know around here?" Sigurd asked, his voice tinged with suspicion.

Why should he care? He didn't have exclusive rights to them, and everything they were doing was by the book. Nothing to hide. Again Abby realized there was little Sigurd could do right by her. She just didn't like him.

"Nope. Didn't even know he was here, until he spotted us," Reid said with an easy drawl.

Abby smiled as Reid did it again. Even more she knew he hadn't warmed to Sigurd either. Which validated her own feelings.

Nevertheless, Abby couldn't trust her instincts right now and even wondered if Hermann was at the top of his game if he was feeling any of the anxiety she was going through.

How could he give up on her? After all, he'd spent the last year making substantial changes to her house on cliffs in Oregon. He'd moved in. Not just his clothes, all of him. The vault, his lab, the elaborate displays. The house was now as much his space as hers. He took great pride in that place.

That thought pulled her back into the moment. "Where do you live, Sigurd? What part of town?" Abby asked suddenly. It seemed important that she saw his house, felt his roots.

"3 Sverres Gate. Not far from here. The reason I came looking for you is that I have an impromptu dinner planned for this evening. In honor of launching the AUV. I know it's short notice, but..." he raised his shoulders in a purely European shrug.

Damn, but he was smooth.

"Thank you. I'm sure we'd all like to see your apartment," Abby answered for them.

"You will be surprised then." His laugh was light, almost indulgent, and rubbed her the wrong way again. She glanced at Hermann; the twinkle in his eyes forced her lips upward into a smile. He knew she was irritated and was telling her to take it easy.

Could he really give up on her?

And maybe you're asking the wrong question.

Abby forced that uncomfortable thought away.

"So, I will see you about seven tonight?" Sigurd glanced at each of them, expecting and receiving a quartet of nods.

He got up and left as abruptly as he arrived.

Abby couldn't wait to see his digs. She'd guess modern, airy and small with Scandinavian furnishings. And she figured they'd dine on takeout food, for he didn't seem the type of guy to cook.

She'd bet on it.

Chapter Ten

The taxi Reid hired to take them to Sigurd's house inched its way down the narrow cobbled street, passing apartments, then small houses and now moving through an area that was filled with large driveways and yards.

Abby sat in the front with the driver, who was signaling to turn into a wide, circular driveway. "Could you stop for a moment before pulling into the drive?"

He stopped at the curb.

They all looked across the street. "This can't be right," Tori said. "I thought you said apartment?"

"This is 3 Sverres Gate," the driver said.

"I thought it would be an apartment." Before them wasn't the typical student abode Abby had assumed. It was a stately multistory house that was well over a century old. Probably older.

Well, damn. She would have lost the bet, had she really made one. And that made her very uncomfortable. Not that she lost, but that she'd pegged Sigurd so incorrectly. Her instinct had failed her.

"It would explain his clothes and his air of superiority," Hermann said.

Abby turned to look at the trio in the back seat and zeroed in on Reid's slight smile. "Did you know?"

He nodded. "Google Earthed it. After you told him it was be nice to see his apartment, I thought I'd let it be a surprise."

Abby rolled her eyes at him and bade the driver enter the wide arc of a paver-laid driveway. Reid paid the driver while they piled out of the taxi.

The house's heavy double doors opened wide and noiselessly on their ancient hinges. Sigurd strode out to meet them before they'd climbed the three steps of the portico. He'd slicked his dark hair back, donned gray tailored slacks, very expensive black shoes, and wore a white shirt opened a couple of buttons at the neck. All in all, Sigurd was the picture of a well-to-do GQ-dressed man.

"Welcome to my home."

"No wonder you laughed when I mentioned apartment. This is a mansion."

"It's been in the family for generations."

He quickly led them through the house with its wood-paneled, portrait-lined walls to the patio.

Abby thought it bit odd that he didn't give them a tour, especially since pride laced his voice when he mentioned how long the family had held the property. She glanced at Hermann and he nodded, understanding her without words.

Then why didn't he understand that the dive

crisis had been an accident? *Perhaps because he knows you better than you know yourself, Abby girl.*

They stepped out of the house onto a brick patio edged with a rough-hewn stone wall that fronted a wide swath of grass bordered by gardens, leading to what she'd guess was the river Nidelva. The same river that cut the city in two and poured its water into the fjord, making diving at times so difficult and dangerous. Damn, was she going to be reminded at every turn about the issue between her and Hermann?

A stunning woman, tall and slender, dressed in a simple black sheath dress with her blonde hair pulled into a chignon, faced the river. She turned to smile at Sigurd as they crossed the patio toward her.

"This is Catherine," their host announced.

He didn't label her as wife, and his voice didn't carry the possessive timbre of a lover. She was just Catherine. Somehow that lack of title bothered Abby. It felt off, dismissive of the woman.

Sigurd took their coats as Catherine greeted each of them by name, pausing a moment when she got to Abby and Tori. She got their names right, but Abby figured it was because Tori was next to Reid and Hermann beside her. Nobody got the twins right on first meeting.

Sigurd had primed her well. Why?

Abby met Tori's gaze as a frisson of caution ran through her. She and her twin had shared this bond as children, this ability to sense danger as well as combine their physical strength when that danger became a reality and they had to fight.

Then they'd grown apart and the bond weakened. Mexico had re-established the link, so when the electricity went through her, she knew something was amiss. Not what exactly, just that something wasn't right here. She nodded slightly, acknowledging Tori's warning.

Abby turned to the table set for six, laid with a pristine table cloth, sterling silver and crystal. Such a show of wealth felt pretentious and somehow fake. As did Catherine.

With sensual grace, the woman moved to an antique wooden sideboard and pulled one of several bottles of wine from a silver cooler filled with ice. She poured five glasses.

"Please enjoy while I go check on the dinner preparations," Sigurd said. "Catherine will keep you company."

The foursome tipped their glasses toward their host and Catherine, then tasted. Abby thought the wine a bit sweet, but utterly delicious.

"Sigurd has told me a bit about your mission. The gold. His desire to return it to the people of Norway," Catherine said.

Her accent wasn't European. Abby was certain she heard a bit of southern drawl. Not as strong as Reid's—he could turn it on thick when needed. More like Catherine was covering it up. Why?

Abby let Hermann talk about their quest as she

surveyed the verdant lawn bordered by a small copse of trees near the river bank. Then something deep in those shadows glinted, reflecting the sunlight from the west, still high in the late Norway evening. Ever the adventurer, the mystery beckoned her to check it out.

She took a step down the patio's steps, then realized she was being incredibly rude. And that realization took her aback. Was her need to be independent turning her into a shrew?

“Catherine, would you mind if I wander around the lower garden? It's so pretty.”

Alarm flared in the woman's eyes and was as quickly dampened. “Of course not. I'll join you.”

Well, damn. Abby didn't want a companion to stop her investigation, and the unease she'd spotted in Catherine's eyes bolstered her determination to see what was in the copse.

“Hermann, would you like to join us?” Abby put as much “keep her away” expression as she could in her gaze, hoping he'd get the message.

“No, I think I'll have another glass of wine,” he said. And successfully diverted their hostess as she veered toward the wooden sideboard and the silver wine cooler to pour him another glass.

Abby flashed him a thank you and continued on her trip down the steps. Wandering around the garden a bit, she moved so she'd be near the copse. Pushing aside branches she stepped into a small, lush forest of pines and ferns, dominated by a five-foot column of stone.

Its surface had been carved with complex, intertwining Norse symbols. Granite slabs set as benches circled the stone, all of it appearing ancient, though recently cleaned of lichen and dirt.

She was standing in front of a rune stone; she was sure of it.

The river was maybe thirty feet from the sanctuary and screened by the trees. Unless you looked closely, you'd never see the stone now, but in ancient days it could have been at the edge of the river. Marking a memorial to an ancestor? Sigurd's ancestor?

Setting her wine glass on one of the benches, Abby slowly circled the stone pillar, trying to discern the weathered symbols. One large, round, intertwined circle caught her eye as the setting sun filtered through the branches and illuminated just that spot.

Her breath caught.

A third sighting of that medallion shape. It had to have more meaning than Reid had found so far. She traced her finger along the chiseled channels of stone. "What are you telling us?" she whispered to the stone, willing it to unlock its secrets.

"I wish I knew."

Abby jumped, thinking for a millisecond that the column had indeed spoken. She whirled around to see Sigurd, holding his own wine glass, a smile lifting one corner of his lips.

"It's magical in here, isn't it? That's why I haven't changed a thing. Except of course to keep the trees and ferns from growing too close to the circle."

He laughed as if at his own sensitivity. "Dinner is to be served in a moment."

"Do you know what the symbols mean?"

"Haven't a clue, except that one," he pointed to the medallion, "must be an ancestral crest. My father never told me anything about what was on the stone. But I liked the shape, so I adopted it. Later, when I have time, I'll get an expert out to read them and tell me for sure."

Abby damped down her excitement and followed Sigurd back to the patio, giving Hermann a smile in answer to his raised brow. Her reveal would have to wait until after they returned to the ship. "I'm sorry to keep everyone waiting," she said, also ignoring Tori's questioning gaze and Catherine's nearly imperceptible frown of concern.

Another surprise followed the moment their host finished seating her. Sigurd had household staff. White-coated waiters brought out small individual platters of cured meats, sausage and dried fruits with a sprig of thyme on each plate. The second course consisted of incredibly tender cod flanked by thick morsels of lobster and thin reeds of baby asparagus.

Sigurd himself served the wine, different for each course. Abby wondered at Catherine's silence. She said little and Sigurd didn't bring her into the conversation. But Abby caught her studying each of them intently, listening carefully to the polite, if stilted, conversation. Sigurd wasn't adept at idle dinner talk.

"And now for the *Bløtkake*, a favorite cake here in Norway," their host announced when a waiter brought out a cake covered in marzipan and topped with fruit.

As Abby bit into it, layers of cream and strawberries melded with the light cake. She followed the bite with a sip of the always strong Norwegian coffee. Heaven.

Clouds gathered, blocking the midnight sun. Lights from the densely clustered buildings across the river created a stunning scene, reflected in the river and off the low-hanging clouds.

The air grew cool enough for Abby to slip on her jacket, as did Tori. The waitstaff set up and turned on outdoor heaters as talk inevitably turned to the AUV's search.

"I know you were disappointed we didn't find the wreckage on the first go around,"—Hermann raised his hands, palms up—"but think how far the plane could have veered from the original coordinates as it fell from the sky. But if the gold is in crates as you suggest, I'm fairly certain they will be near the wreckage."

"And the AUV is still down there doing its work, even with the *Brizo* back at port," Reid added.

Sigurd sat back in his chair, appearing almost as lord of the manor. He only needed to steeple his fingers under his chin and the picture would be complete, Abby thought. Quite different in attitude from the cautious, rich grad student who came to them less than a week ago. Who was the real Sigurd?

"I'm quite sure we'll find it. It is only day one, no? We have a bit more time." Sigurd waved his arm languidly as if it didn't matter. But the hardness in his eyes told a different story.

"A bit?" Reid repeated. "I didn't realize we were working on a specific time frame here."

"You mistake my words. I merely meant that time marches on, and I'm quite sure you wish to return to your honeymoon, eh?"

Abby wondered what Sigurd would have said if she'd brought up his comment. He answer felt glib, as usual.

"Oh, Sigurd, a honeymoon doesn't end with its location," Tori said with a slight, secret smile.

Jealousy bit Abby, then she brushed the emotion aside, knowing this joy could be hers as well if she just . . . what?

"Tomorrow begins in an hour. We should be heading back to the ship. Thank you for an incredible meal. Someday you must give us a tour of your house." Hermann rose.

"Let me take you back. It's late for a taxi."

Piling into Sigurd's Mercedes station wagon, parked at the side of the driveway—no going back into the house for them—they zipped through the streets of Trondheim, still filled with late night partygoers. The bridge over the Nidelva was brightly lit and the city wore a festive air.

Sigurd dropped them off on the pier and watched until they walked up the gangway, then drove off.

Tori was about to say something when Hermann put a finger to her lips. “It was a good evening and the food delicious,” he said loudly.

Abby smiled while Tori gave him a blank look. Reid winked and carefully checked the pockets of Tori's jacket, then the lining, and shook his head.

***

Closing the door to the mess, Hermann leaned against it. “We're clear. Captain Andrews swept the ship and his berth before we returned.”

“What was that all about?” Tori voice was as bewildered as her gaze. “And swept the ship as in for listening devices?”

“Yeah. And I was checking to see if the son of a bitch bugged you,” Reid said, a touch of anger lacing his voice. “He didn't, but both Hermann and I were pretty sure he was going to try.”

“Why me?”

“You're the only one who wouldn't know what the thing looked like if you'd found it.” Hermann looked apologetically at her. “He'd know you were the neophyte among us.”

“I think I need a crash course in field work. This is different than what happened in Mexico,” Tori said.

“Darlin', they're all different.” Reid wrapped her in a hug.

"That's what keeps us on our toes," Abby added. "Speaking of which . . . " She rocked on her toes with excitement.

Hermann grinned. This was what had drawn him to her in the first place. Her love for adventure. Was he right asking her to change? No, not change but be more respectful of the danger she put herself in. To think of the other people in her life. This business they were in was dangerous enough. She didn't need to take greater risks, prove to herself that she was invincible. He'd threatened to leave her, but could he really?

Can you watch her die?

No. Not by taking unnecessary risks.

Her eyes lit with excitement, and his heart beat faster.

But you can take this moment right now and hope she'll see the light before you have the conversation you promised her.

He wrapped an arm around her and for a split second felt her stiffen, then relax.

"In the copse of trees I found a rune stone with benches around it. And carved on the stone was the same medallion shape as on Sigurd's laptop and Magnus's photo frame," Abby said, her words tumbling over themselves. "I asked Sigurd if he knew the meaning of any of the symbols and he said no, but he would get an expert out when he had time. That man always has an answer for everything."

"He's slick. Notice how he had the car parked

so we wouldn't have to walk back through the house? Got to wonder why." Reid worked his phone as he talked.

Hermann wouldn't have guessed he'd ever like Reid after the China incident, let alone admire him, yet he did. It also surprised him that Tori had changed so much since Mexico, but she had. And frankly, they were the perfect couple. Different enough to keep each other on their toes. They respected each other, and their love was obviously deep.

"Okay then, stop me if I'm wrong. Sigurd had the symbol on his laptop, and on a Rune Stone at his house, and Magnus had it on his frame. Is it at all possible they're connected as family?"

Hermann stared at Tori. "You may well be onto another angle we'd not considered."

"I'm not sure I'd want to have Sigurd as kin," Abby said.

Except for the tapping of Reid's fingers on his phone, the mess was silent.

"Still no connection. Went back a few genealogical levels."

"I don't think we should let Magnus in on our discovery yet. He said he wanted to look up church records, so let's offer to help him and start with Nidaros Cathedral," Abby said.

"Why there?"

"It's very close to 3 Sverres Gate and it's the biggest in the city."

"How do you know that?" Tori asked.

"I always do research on a place before I go there. Always."

Hermann heard the defensive tone in Abby's voice and squeezed her shoulders. He was rewarded with a smile that stung his heart.

Reid finished tapping on his keyboard. "There is a large cemetery at Nidaros. I didn't see a current plot map, but there's one from 1879. A number of Thorsens are listed there, but no Joneses."

"Maybe we can find a first name of Brigitte in the records. So let's see if we can convince him to look with us. We're a bit off our treasure hunt here, but I liked Magnus and we can afford to spend the time while the AUV is doing its search. And maybe it'll help him find his ancestors."

"I think that's an excellent idea, Tori. And if they are family, it may also give us better insight into Sigurd, who seems more of a puzzle than ever," Hermann said. The man bothered him still. His exhaustive dossiers on each of them felt sinister. And there was subtext in nearly every conversation they'd had with him.

Actually he hoped Sigurd and Magnus weren't related. But there could be some other connection. Hermann felt the medallion image's meant something and both men had it.

Chapter Eleven

Returning home after delivering his dinner guests to their boat, Sigurd moved to his library, sinking into the deep leather club chair. On the mahogany table next to him Catherine had set out the crystal decanter with his favorite aged-to-perfection brandy and a single glass.

Running a finger across the aged smoothness of the wood and then the chiseled facets of the decanter, he appreciated the juxtaposition of the two textures. Much like his life. Luxury clashing with the tension of his mission.

Sigurd poured a generous measure and gently swirled the golden liquor in the heavy crystal snifter as he replayed the evening and the one snafu.

He'd watched Abby throughout their meal, catching her gaze darting to the copse more than once.

He knew she'd figured out that the carving on the rune stone was the same image she'd glimpsed on his computer back in Oregon. That had been a slip. But he was pretty sure she'd bought his story of it being a family crest. And he was certain his impromptu explanation clarified the reason for the image of the medallion she'd spied on his laptop screen in Oregon.

Anyway, this was a little mistake that wouldn't need to be reported. It was only an inconvenience. And he felt his smokescreen was still intact.

Nevertheless, his grip tightened on the bowl of the snifter. Too many little mistakes and a crisis would emerge.

Where was Catherine? His body ached in anticipation of her adeptness at making him forget everything but the feel of her hands, the silky roughness of her tongue.

He groaned softly. She was the perk of being Number One at the Table of One Hundred, and he wondered what the perks would be when he was promoted to the Table of Three and was second only to Peter Schwartz.

Feeling itchy, unsettled and needing Catherine, a need he felt showed dependence, he countered that weakness by calling his lieutenant.

"None of the four are to be out of the sight of your men at any time, and be careful—these are not novices and they will detect you. I reiterate, make no moves unless approved by me. Watch and record every bit of information, no matter how trivial. Are you certain of your latest recruits? They are untested," he said, voice sharp.

"Sir, they have passed all testing at the compound's training facility. They are loyal to the cause and received the highest marks," his lieutenant responded. "Your mission has priority."

Which should have made Sigurd feel better. But he noticed while at the compound earlier this year, the men and woman being trained now tended to be trigger happy and prone to letting force become the first line of questioning.

"Be certain or . . . " He let his words hang. His lieutenant knew exactly the cost of failure, as he himself did.

Catherine slipped into the room, and he abruptly hung up the phone, anxious for the relief he'd soon receive.

Chapter Twelve

Before hitting their room at the hotel in the wee hours of the night, Reid and Tori found Magnus in the Sky Bar. He agreed to come with them to the Nidaros Cathedral to start researching his grandmother Brigitte's name on a birth registry. They didn't mention their quest of looking up the name Thorsen.

The next morning, Magnus was waiting at the entrance to the hotel. Reid signaled a taxi and the three of them piled in. "Nidaros Cathedral," he instructed the driver.

As the taxi wound its way up the long driveway, they passed the cathedral's lush ancient cemetery, filled with old trees blooming, for spring came late to Norway. Shaggy, verdant grass stretched like a carpet between the grave markers.

The cathedral itself loomed above the cemetery in all its medieval majesty.

Reid, Tori, and Magnus entered through the west nave of the Cathedral and followed a tour group until they stopped to take pictures of the enormous and deeply impressive rose window over a huge pipe organ.

"You know, I think I preferred the church in Tenosique, simple but filled with grace," Reid whispered.

Tori glanced at her husband, surprised at his sensitivity. She felt the same way. And she missed Sister Angelique.

Approaching the near-by guide, Tori smiled at her and received a beaming smile in return. "If you have a second, can you point us in the direction of the records office?"

"You want the Archives house, back out and to the left."

"Thank you," Magnus said.

Only to have the young woman grin wider. That man had a way with women, Tori thought as they headed out of the Cathedral.

"Shades of Tenosique," Reid said once they were outside.

"What is Tenosique?" Magnus asked.

"A wonderful little town in Mexico where we looked for clues in the church."

"Let's hope your luck holds."

They found the office, and the secretary told them it would take her a bit of time to pull the volumes from the 1930s to the 1950s.

"Is there a caretaker of the cemetery we could talk to while we wait?" Tori asked.

"Henri has a small cottage on the grounds."

They walked back into the sunshine and around the massive cathedral to the burial grounds.

Before reaching the cottage, they found Henri bent over a hoe, clearing out weeds. He was far younger than Tori had hoped. He was around Magnus's age and wouldn't know anything first-hand about the 1940s.

"Henri?"

His nod was less than welcoming, but that didn't dissuade her from pushing past his reserve.

"Tori and Reid Hunter," she introduced, loving the way her married name rolled off her tongue. It felt so right.

"The secretary in the Archives office mentioned you and we're trying to find some family history."

Henri lifted one shoulder and appeared less than interested.

Not the most communicative man on the planet, Tori thought, figuring this was a dead end.

Magnus stepped forward. "Magnus Jones, sir." He reached out to shake Henri's hand.

"Dirty."

"I'm used to it. My mother had a huge garden, and the weeds were my job." Magnus shrugged and kept his hand out.

Henri didn't smile or frown but did shake it.

Tori guessed they'd passed some sort of test.

Magnus stepped back and stumbled over a root. He flailed his arms, trying to keep his balance, failed, and Tori caught him just before he hit the ground.

She realized that both Henri and Magnus would wonder about her enhanced reflexes, so she'd need to come up with a story, fast.

But Henri wasn't paying her any attention. He was focused on the leather frame that had dropped out of Magnus's pocket.

"Where did you get that?" he asked in a voice tight with urgency.

"It was my mother's."

Henri carefully picked up the frame and traced the embossed symbol on its cover. "Follow me," he said with an odd note of urgency, and started off across the tall grass.

Magnus followed Henri without hesitation for a few yards, then paused and shot them a questioning glance over his shoulder.

"I guess we should do as ordered," she said, getting a nod from Reid.

They quickly caught up with Magnus and Henri as he led them deeper into the cemetery. Away from the busyness of the Cathedral to a small stone cottage, its window shutters closed, looking as if they had been that way for years.

They entered the main room, which was filled with shelves of books and two comfortable chairs with a reading lamp for each one. Sitting in one of the recliners was a wizened man, asleep, softly snoring. An open book lay across his chest.

"Grandfather, wake up, now please."

"La en gammel mann søvn," he muttered in Norse.

"Grandfather, you'll sleep the whole day away, and these people are the ones you've waited for." Henri turned toward them with an apologetic expression in his eyes. "He speaks good English, just refuses to unless he knows why he should bother."

Waited for?

His eyes opened, and Tori expected a pale blue, like Henri's, but the old man before them had rich blue eyes, filled with sleep from his nap.

Henri brought him a glass of water. "I'm sorry I can't offer you a place to sit. We never have visitors here."

Thus the closed shutters, Tori thought.

"We won't stay long," Magnus assured him. He pulled out the leather frame again and handed it to the old man.

"I'm Magnus Jones, and this came from my mother, Cindy Jones. The pictures are of her and her mother, Brigitte Jones."

The man took the leather frame. His eyes widened as he traced the embossed leather. Then he flipped open the frame and gazed at both pictures, then up at Magnus. "This is your grandmother?" he said in heavily accented English, pointing to the picture of Brigitte.

The urgency in his voice puzzled Tori. This was simply a quest to find roots. She glanced at Reid and saw the questioning frown on his forehead as he stared intently at the leather frame in the old man's hands.

"Yes, it is. And my mother is on her lap."

Tori watched as gnarled fingers felt along the edge of the frame, then pushed into two places simultaneously.

Brigitte's picture swung open like the page of a book, and nestled below it was a small medallion of gold with the same interwoven image as was embossed on the leather case. The same as the rune stone and the image on Sigurd's computer.

***

Magnus's gasp rang loudly in the small stone cottage. "What the hell is that?" He reached out, but the old man snapped shut the secret compartment.

He handed back the frame to Magnus. "Before you hold the medallion, you should know the truth," he said. "There are things I must show you, to help you understand." He nodded to Henri, who left the room at a run.

The old man struggled to get out of his big chair.

Magnus and Reid flanked the chair, helping him up, and the three men, with Tori close behind, headed for the door. Outside, Henri was ready with a small electric cart with room for two. And he had a wicked looking semi-automatic handgun on his lap.

Tori stared at it, then at Reid and saw his concern over the fact that Henri apparently needed a gun wherever they were headed.

Then she finally glanced at Magnus, who

looked shocked and confused. Tori couldn't blame him as she felt the same way.

They helped the old man into the cart; he pointed and Henri started off.

Tori, Reid and Magnus jogged behind the cart.

"Faster," the grandfather urged.

"Go, we'll keep up," Reid called to them.

Tori broke into a fast run, then remembered to slow down as she led the trio. Reid kept Magnus in the middle and brought up the rear.

Stopping by a messy clump of bushes, Henri helped his grandfather out of the cart, then tucked the gun in the waistband of his khaki work pants.

"Grandfather has never allowed me to clean up this area."

Pushing lightly through the tangle of branches and high grass, they followed the old man, who seemed to get stronger and more upset the deeper they penetrated the mess. Actually it was only about fifty feet, but it felt like another world. Much like Tulum in their Yucatan quest.

"Are your adventures always like this?" she whispered to Reid.

His shrug said it all.

The old man stopped before a lichen-encrusted slab of granite. Six feet in height and the width of a man, it looked like a huge headstone. Scraping at the crusty growth with an old pocket knife, he revealed the same crest as on the frame. He continued to work on what looked like an inscription, and finally got it clean enough to read.

"The family Ødegård, betrayed in life, safe in death," the old man read softly.

Tori's heart beat faster as tears welled in his eyes.

"I've been waiting for you. This is your family, I believe," he whispered in English. "All but one perished, and she was sent away for safety. A child who'd died a few days before in the hospital took her place in the house where it all happened."

"They were murdered?" Magnus asked, horror trembling in his voice.

"They were. Running away was not an option. It was war time and your great grandfather also knew once they'd been discovered, they'd be looking over their shoulder the rest of their lives. I would call it a sacrifice to protect that." The old man nodded to the leather frame Magnus held. "It has been an Ødegård's job to protect the medallion and the gold from the beginning.

"You are your great grandfather's namesake. He was my friend and though I was only a young man of sixteen, he trusted me. Once he realized he'd been betrayed, he swiftly created a plan I was to carry out regarding gold and the Nazis, but more importantly, he needed me to make sure the centuries-old secret remained safe. He entrusted his young daughter's fate with me. I was to send Brigitte far away, along with the secret in the frame."

The old man bowed his head for a moment, then stood taller

"I knew he'd planned to sacrifice his and his wife Astrid's lives to make it look like all, including their daughter, had perished and the secret with them. And I didn't try to change his mind. It would have done no good. He was bitter with grief over being taken in by his good friend. But the secret had to remain safe. That was his lifelong task."

"Who was his friend? And what secret?" Magnus asked.

Tori heard the confusion, the shock in his voice. So much had been revealed in short order.

They heard a rustle in the trees beyond their hiding place, followed by the loud flapping of a multitude of wings. A flock of birds had been disturbed.

The old man stopped talking immediately and looked upward. "The trees have grown too close. I did not realize. We must finish this conversation in the cottage. You will return and cover our tracks," he ordered Henri in a whisper. Then he seemed to deflate; all the energy fled his body and he sagged. Reid and Magnus supported him as they walked back through the tangle of branches to the cart.

Henri emerged first, gun at the ready, followed by the trio of men with Tori bringing up the rear. She wanted to study the stone longer but felt the urgency in the old man's words. They needed to leave.

"He's got a gun," a woman screamed.

They all turned toward the voice, seeing a trio of women standing next to a nearby headstone, thinking they were screaming about Henri's gun.

Instead one woman pointed upward at a tree. Tori saw a shadowy figure in the branches and turned to push everyone back into the shelter of the tangled bushes.

Suddenly the old man jerked backward, blood pouring from his chest. A split second later he jerked again and collapsed to the ground.

Henri immediately dropped to a knee beside him, gun aiming at the canopy of green.

The air whooshed from Tori's chest as Reid flung her face-down into the grass, covering her body with his own.

Magnus cradled the old man as Henri crouched beside them, scanning the area.

They were pinned down and easy pickings.

***

Reid, still protecting Tori with his own body, lay absolutely still and listened intently. He heard nothing, no birdsong, no scraping of feet down tree branches, or footfalls running on the grass.

He gingerly lifted his head and looked at the tree the woman had pointed to and saw nothing. Then he looked at the woman beneath him. “Darlin', you okay?”

“Yep, let me up. Henri's grandfather . . . ”

He climbed off Tori, and they bent over the old man cradled in Magnus's arms. Henri had abandoned his gun and was leaning close to his grandfather's lips.

The old man opened his eyes and mouthed

something in Norse, then breathed no more.

Henri gently closed his grandfather's eyes, and sat back on his heels, head bowed for a moment.

Reid said a silent prayer for both of them.

"He said, 'You've been found,'" Henri said, pain lacing each word.

Magnus looked up from the body still held in his arms. "We have to call the authorities."

"No."

"No? Your grandfather has just been murdered."

"He was already dead."

Reid looked sharply at Henri. "That needs an explanation—"

"Please help me pull him into the bushes, then I will explain. And after you leave, I will attend to my *bestefar*."

Reid and Magnus refused to pull the wizened old man across the ground, instead lifting his light weight gently and, with great care, carried him back to the stone in the tangle of bushes and trees.

"I will say this quickly, and you must go. Grandfather faked his death shortly after the war. His duty, my father's duty and mine have always been clear. We were to watch for an Ødegård to return."

Magnus looked beyond stunned. "And I'm an Ødegård? You're sure?"

"Grandfather was sure. And now they will come after it."

"They?"

"Those who belong to the SineQuaNon. The remaining Nazis I should think, but we were never sure. My task is to explain that the medallion has power, a connection to Odin himself. Which is why they wanted it so long ago and now obviously still do. The medallion was King Olaf's until he converted and ordered it destroyed. According to legend, the Ødegårds were entrusted with keeping the medallion and the gold safe. You must continue this. If you need the power beyond what you can muster yourself, the gold will help.

"This is all I know—you must go, and I'll see that Grandfather is buried in the grave he himself dug so long ago. Take this and my job is over." He pulled a chain from around his grandfather's neck. From it dangled a small key. The old man's blood covered both the chain and the key. "It opens the vault—"

Sirens sounded too close for comfort.

"Go."

"But you—"

"I'll take care of grandfather and then disappear. My job is over. Go, don't let his death be in vain."

Chapter Thirteen

Reid was chillingly aware that if the shooter was still in the cemetery, the public setting wouldn't ensure their safety. Even with the three of them sprinting and dodging, using the cemetery's headstones for protection, they could still become victims of a bullet.

The siren's wail grew louder, which meant they needed to leave now, but also that the shooter would be fleeing as well—but in which direction? Would they run into him?

Reid made swift eye contact with Tori and saw the trust in her eyes. Magnus's gaze was darting wildly between the bushes and the body near his family's obelisk, and Reid couldn't get his attention.

"Okay, stay tight together. We're heading for the street and a cab," he instructed the two he needed to protect. With one more sorrowful glance at Henri and his lifeless grandfather, Reid grabbed Tori's hand tightly and started off running fast, weaving around tombstones, hoping his idea of creating difficult targets would work.

He looked back once to make sure Magnus was close on their heels.

He wasn't.

Stopping next to a large headstone, Reid pushed Tori down behind it and crouched beside her, scanning the area, trying to get a glimpse of the direction Magnus was heading.

Zero.

"Damn."

"What, the shooter?"

"No, Magnus. He ran the other way. I can't see him."

"Probably ready to jump the next flight to the US and bury himself in his work."

"He's in danger, that's the exact wrong thing to do . . . "

"I know."

Of course she did. "Are you okay?" he asked the woman he loved more than his own life.

Tori's laugh was shaky but there. "Okay. But this—" She lifted her shoulders. "How do you stand it?"

"Part is the rush of beating the odds, finding the unfindable. But I gotta admit, Darlin', the last three hunts, from China to today, have tested even me. Too much death."

Tori nodded, and he was so grateful she understood. He didn't have to go into exhaustive detail. She simply got it. Got him.

Craning his neck, he saw the main thoroughfare, only about twenty-five yards away.

"Ready for one more dash? Then we'll snag a cab back to the *Brizo*."

As an answer, she grabbed his hand, pulling him up, and took the lead.

They reached the street and slowed, melding with the crowds.

"Flag a cab while I call Hermann," he said.

"Where are we going? Returning to the *Brizo* will put them all in danger."

"Right now, we're just getting away from here."

As he waited impatiently for the two rings it took for Hermann to pick up, Reid scanned the busy intersection. Nothing looked off, but there were too many people to be certain.

Finally Hermann answered.

"Things just got dicey. Shot at, one down, none of us, but Magnus is on the run, scared. Nazis may be involved. Put the ship on alert. Heading—"

"Come here. I'll double the guard immediately," Hermann said.

A taxi stopped, and Reid motioned for Tori to get in. "On our way," Reid said, hanging up. "The pier in front of the Rockheim," he told the driver.

Tori's fingers grasped his, and he raised their joined hands to his lips, earning a wan smile in return.

Maybe it was time to give up this life. Betrayal and danger were commonplace in this biz, but the lethal threat had rarely come from other mortals. Nature had been the greater foe.

When he'd partnered with Abby, mostly they

dealt with misdirection, natural dangers and greasing palms. Then the China gig and the ultimate betrayal that nearly cost Hermann his life, while it had destroyed everyone's trust in Reid. His response had been typical of the Hunter blood that ran through him. Screw 'em if they thought so little of his integrity.

Then Tori came into his life, and suddenly it mattered what people thought of him. It took awhile and a lot of convincing, with people coming forward after having their palms plied with payola, but the truth won.

He won.

And now this. China, Mexico and Norway. They all wanted a piece of him and worse, of the people he loved.

The taxi fought through the midday crowds and traffic, finally reaching the Rockheim. Hermann was on deck along with Captain Andrews, who now wore a nylon shoulder harness with a Sig Sauer 9mm tucked in its holster. Two additional men Reid didn't recognize were in position on the bow and stern of the *Brizo*. Hermann obviously worked his magic fast.

Leaving the taxi, Reid again grabbed Tori's hand as they ran toward the safety of the ship. He made Tori go first while he backed across the gangway behind her as a shield.

All was quiet.

Reid wanted them out of view and practically pushed Tori into the shelter of the passage leading into the mess. Abby barely let them step foot into the room before Tori was enveloped in a hug. Then Reid got his.

"What happened? God, you're covered with grass and dirt. Hermann mentioned gunfire? At the cathedral?"

Hermann entered the mess along with Captain Andrews, then closed the passage door behind them. But not before Reid saw that one of the same men who had been on deck now guarded the door.

Captain Andrews lowered the shades over the starboard side windows, then stood near the stairways. Hermann was taking no chances.

"Magnus bolted. He's in danger—"

Hermann moved to the door and spoke with the man there, then returned to the table. "I've sent people to the hotel to watch for him. Then bring him here."

"I'm guessing whoever shot at us wants the medallion he carries." Reid quickly described the events at the cathedral and the basic information revealed by Henri's grandfather. "There is no doubt they'll kill Magnus for it."

"They'll have to go through my men first."

Reid nodded, knowing that to be absolutely true. "Have you heard of the SineQuaNon before?" he asked.

Hermann stilled. "How do they play into this?"

The hairs on the back of Reid's neck quivered. He was stunned at the low fury vibrating in Hermann's voice. He saw the same shock on the twin's faces. Captain Andrews looked unperturbed.

"You know of them."

"Ja."

Crap. "And you're not involved."

"Never."

Reid met Hermann's eyes, and despite the conviction in his voice, Reid saw a flicker of elusiveness in his eyes. It appeared that even Abby noticed his hesitation in answering the question as she too searched his face.

"Okay." It was all Reid could do, drop the matter, for now. "Magnus learned today that he is a descendant of the Ødegård family, an ancient lineage, from what we gathered."

Reid looked at Tori to see if she agreed. She nodded.

"The medallion may have the power of Odin attached to it in some way and apparently came from King Olaf. The old man that was killed today had pledged to keep the Ødegård's secret, and now his son will. He said he was prepared to disappear, and I'm sure he will and has fled."

"The secret being?" Abby asked.

"That the medallion still exists. King Olaf ordered it destroyed, either because he'd converted to Christianity or because it does hold power and in the wrong hands—"

"The SineQuaNon wants it for the power it possesses," Hermann said simply.

***

A knock on the mess door stopped all

conversation.

Captain Andrews stood with his hand on his holster as Hermann slid the pocket door open. Magnus, flanked by two of the Captain's men, stood pale and trembling, glancing about in confusion.

“You're putting everyone in danger by bringing me here,” he said, his voice tight with fear.

“Hermann has extra people to protect us. Come sit down,” Abby said, scooting over on the banquette to make room for him. “We were just discussing the medallion and Odin's power—”

“Odin is a myth,” Magnus interrupted.

Abby couldn't help the gentle laughter that bubbled up, joined in by Tori and Reid. Hermann refrained.

“Magnus, many of the things we've found *and* held were myths at one time. That's what makes this so interesting. That's why we laughed, not at you or the situation.”

“Someone has already died. I don't want more blood on my hands. And what the hell is the Sign Q something the old man talked about?”

“SineQuaNon as in Sin-neh, Qua, Non,” Hermann pronounced. “The SineQuaNon's closest translation means “without, there is no existence.” People use the phrase for many different things. This SineQuaNon is a secret society created after King Olaf's conversion.”

“You mean like the Templar knights?” Tori asked.

“More like opposites,” Reid said. “I couldn't believe my ears when I heard Henri's grandfather mention that name. I thought they were more myth than real.” He shrugged. “I fell into my own trap of not believing, and I've seen my share of the unbelievable. So believe me, Magnus, I understand your confusion.”

After seeing that he had the young man’s attention, Reid continued. “The Knights Templar gave their money to charity when they joined the organization; the SineQuaNon members give their wealth to their society.”

“What do they control?” Abby directed her question to Hermann.

“Politics, banking, stock markets. There is a table of three, then below that, the table of one hundred.”

Abby kept her focus on Hermann, who looked fiercely worried. “You know a lot about this group?”

Hermann nodded.

Not his usual way of admitting anything. He was direct and outspoken whether he was in the right or admitting wrong.

“I'm sensing we have more than a treasure hunt on our hands,” Abby said.

“No. I'm not going to involve you in this any further. I'll go into hiding.” Magnus rose from the table. “And I'll bury the medallion so no one will find it.”

“And then you'll be tortured until you give up

the location. They *will* find you, and they will find the location of the medallion, now that they know an Ødegård lives," Hermann said.

Magnus sat back, stunned.

"Your great grandfather believed that as well, apparently," Tori said.

"Can we fight the SineQuaNon?" Abby asked.

"Ja."

"Can we win?"

"Perhaps, or perhaps not. We can win battles, but I am uncertain if we can destroy them," Hermann said softly.

"I'm stunned by your saying that. We beat the damned Believers and their immortal god, for cripes sakes," Reid said as Abby watched him grasp Tori's hand and hold it tightly.

"But this is more, isn't it?" Abby looked squarely at Hermann. There was more than just his knowing about the SineQuaNon.

"It may be," he admitted. "I know we're safest on the ship. And I think we should continue on with our quest."

"I believe there is a connection between the gold on the wreck and the brooch," Reid said. "Before Magnus joined us, I was about to mention that Henri had said 'the gold will help'. I think the gold in that Nazi plane was the same gold taken from the Ødegårds."

"And Sigurd? Does he play into this?" Abby hadn't liked the guy from the get-go, and while that wasn't an odd reaction to have about an outside partner in this oft secret world of treasure hunting, maybe her instincts were playing out about him.

"I think there is little doubt he's involved. The symbol has been seen twice connected with him," Hermann said. "To advance up the ranks of the SineQuaNon, one is given a task to find an object of great power. Sometimes the task takes generations of a family."

"Then the symbol I saw on the rune stone at Sigurd's house could that be related to the fact they've been hunting for it for generations?"

"I think it adds one more tick to the plus column that Sigurd is SineQuaNon. But I'd like irrefutable proof. Which is why I think we should continue on here as if we know nothing." Hermann turned to Magnus. "Keeping the medallion on your person is . . . risky. Would you allow me to put it in a place of safekeeping?"

Magnus held out the leather photo wallet and fumbled with the edges.

"How is it supposed to open?" Abby asked, taking pity on him and holding out her hand for the frame. He was shaking too hard to make anything work.

Magnus handed her the frame. "The old man ran his finger on the edge, found something and pressed it."

"Okay, I feel one slightly raised bump." She pressed it and nothing happened.

"I think I remember that the frame was open and then he pressed two places," Tori said.

Abby opened the frame, then ran her finger along the lower edge. "Got it, it's really almost impossible to feel the bump." She pressed both simultaneously and Brigitte's picture swung upward, revealing the medallion.

No larger than a half dollar in size, it looked thin and brittle, with light hammer marks on the gold, perhaps forged by Odin himself. Abby wanted to pick it up, but it wasn't hers to hold, and Magnus stared at it like a rabbit held captive by a snake.

With great care she handed him the frame back, and he gingerly picked up the medallion

The moment he touched the gold, his fingers clenched and his arm twitched involuntarily.

Then all was still.

"You are a conduit, Mr. Ødegård," Hermann said solemnly.

"That's not my last name. What the hell does that mean? Why me?"

"From what I know of the *myth,* as you called it, Odin was furious that King Olaf would dare order his gift destroyed. Odin deceptively guided the King's choice of family to destroy the medallion, and Odin helped the original Ødegård make it look as if it had been destroyed," Reid said. "He then gave the power of the medallion to the clan of Ødegårds. I have no idea what specific power the medallion holds. Nor am I sure about the gold and its history. But I am pretty damn sure that the power will be yours when you call upon it."

***

In the quiet after Reid's pronouncement, Hermann studied Magnus, concerned that he might refuse the gift of Odin's power. That would be a disastrous choice. “Do you have any family?”

All eyes turned toward Hermann, except Captain Andrews’s. Hermann had primed him that once Magnus was found, he should be watched carefully. The young man was untested and thus an unknown quantity. Hermann relied on Andrews to watch for slips, for artificial answers, for anything that might indicate Magnus couldn't be trusted to follow crucial instructions, or worse, that he might betray them to save his own life. Hermann knew the captain's stint as a Lord Commissioner of Justiciary in Scotland served him well in reading people.

The younger man looked up from the medallion sitting in his hands. “No, none. Not married, no time or money to date. Nothing.”

“Then this is good. The SineQuaNon will use anything and anyone to gain the advantage. That means, had you a wife or children, they would be in danger.

“That also means anyone associated with you is in danger. Meaning us. You were correct in that earlier supposition. May I?” Hermann held out his hand.

Magnus placed the gold in his palm and Hermann gripped it.

Nothing. He passed it to Abby. Nothing. Same with Reid. But when Tori held it, her arm quivered.

Hermann had expected that, after all she was stronger and faster now because of the blue jade in her body. Perhaps all mystical powers connected to each other. Isn't that what the SineQuaNon wanted with all they'd collected through the centuries?

He wondered what it would have done in Alfred's palm. He had strengths and a connection to something none of them knew about. It unsettled Hermann that he didn't know, but he was also certain they'd find out at the point Alfred wanted them to.

Tori passed the medallion back to Magnus. "I think you may need this sometime soon, but I agree with Hermann—it's best to keep it hidden. When you are ready for it, it will know, and you'll master the power," she counseled.

Reid and Abby blinked at Tori's response, while Hermann grinned, for the first time since Reid called from the cemetery shooting. This Tori wasn't the same person he'd met on the narrow ledge of El Castillo in Mexico.

"Hey, you guys, don't look so surprised," she said. "I had to learn to temper my strength and speed now that I have that jade inside me. Otherwise, I'd break fingers when I shook hands, or outpace everyone when we were supposed to be strolling along. I even bent a bracelet too much when I was simply trying to hold it against the mandrel to form it."

"What is it with you all? You have superpowers, deal with secret societies, uncover myths that aren't, but instead are real, and find objects that hold their own special powers." Magnus's voice rose on each word.

"Herr Jones," Hermann didn't want to upset him more using his real last name of Ødegård. He gave Magnus the gist of the search for the stone of heaven and what happened to Tori. "So, with the exception of Tori, we've been at this for a good while, so it doesn't seem odd to us to see these things. Technology has changed this game; news of any kind can flash around the world in minutes, and be acted on for good or bad. But back when we started—"

Reid interrupted, "The danger didn't seem as risky as it does now—"

"And as Hermann has often said, to find the unfindable is what it's about, and frankly it's a rush I can't imagine living without," Abby's voice rang with enthusiasm.

Hermann mustered his best acting skills to hide the immense pain he felt at Abby's words. He caught the stricken look in her eyes the moment the words left her mouth. But he couldn't ignore that the sentiment came straight from her heart. The woman was an adventure junkie, and he knew one day she'd go too far. He didn't know what drove her to gamble with her life , but he hated that it had hold of her and not even his love could release its tentacles.

Hermann saw a look pass between Reid and Tori. They got it too, and even if they didn't know what was going on between Abby and himself, both of them knew of the crazy risks she took.

"Okay, a little change of focus," Reid said. "Back at the cemetery, Henri handed you a key. Do you still have it?"

Magnus pulled it out of his pocket, still stained with the old man's blood. He wet his napkin from the bottled water that was as ever-present as the coffee cups at the table and wiped off the blood. "After the old man died, Henri said it was their family's task to watch for an Ødegård and that this key opened a vault. But the rest of what he was going to say was cut off because the police sirens were too close and he needed to take care of his grandfather's . . . body."

The key was small, so it could be hidden or worn, Hermann guessed.

"Are you still in agreement that this should be kept in a safe place until we're clear of—"

"When will that be? Sounds like maybe never. Anyway, are you sure you don't want me to keep it? I'd be the only one to die if they found it."

"No, frankly you wouldn't, as I explained earlier. And keeping it out of the wrong hands is paramount." Hermann watched as Magnus mechanically but methodically placed the gold back into its niche inside the leather picture frame, with the key on top, and folded down the picture of Brigitte. The young man closed the frame and handed it to him.

Slipping out of the room, followed by Captain

Andrews, who then waited outside the master cabin, Hermann put the worn frame in the safe under the bed, intensely curious about what the key unlocked. He figured they'd find out sooner rather than later if the SineQuaNon was involved.

And if they were, they would fight this battle. If they won, he and Alfred alone would fight the next one. There was no way he'd involve Abby, Tori or Reid in that war.

He wished he'd followed his first instinct to walk away when he'd felt that twinge of unease when Sigurd had pinged him with too much information, but he'd ignored it. Then he realized he probably wouldn't have been able to refuse this quest. If Sigurd was indeed in the SineQuaNon, he'd have found leverage to make Hermann recover the gold.

Which would have been Abby, and most probably Tori and Reid.

Sigurd's mistake, of course, was to believe the medallion was with the gold at the bottom of the fjord.

Chapter Fourteen

Sigurd sat on one of the granite slabs that circled the rune stone in the copse on the grounds of the mansion at 3 Sverres Gate. He turned up the volume on his MP3 player, letting the passion and darkness of Orff's *Carmina Burana* run through him. Filling him with strength and focus. Unlike the lyrics, fate would not play a hand in this operation. He had it planned to the last detail.

The little irritations like Abby Carswell intruding into this spot and seeing the stone were simply that, small annoyances.

Nevertheless, his calm was constantly being disrupted by these people. And had they not been the only ones whom he needed, he wouldn't have wasted another thought on them.

Sigurd had figured approaching them and using the lure of a grand adventure was the better way to snag their cooperation, but now he wondered if he should have taken Abby, Tori and Reid hostage to ensure Hermann did his bidding.

Then again, had he tipped his hand in the

beginning, he'd have had the sworn enemies of the SineQuaNon on him in a flash and would have had to fight that battle first.

He'd taken the right action, even if at times these people tested his conviction.

Pulling a stack of photos from his leather portfolio, he held and studied each 8 by 10 photo. Even though he'd memorized them, seeing them again soothed his irritation at the same time it increased his anticipation.

The black and white photos showed immeasurable wealth. Hundreds of gold arm bands, helmet pieces, circlets worn as crowns for ceremony, women's girdle chains and coins were laid out on every imaginable surface, even on the silk rugs on the floor of the library in the very house he now occupied. Pictures of the spoils the Nazis were bringing home to Mother Germany.

Then, once the treasures reached Germany, Sigurd's great grandfather, a high-ranking figure in the Nazi party, had been in a position to spirit the treasures away. At least that was the plan. Instead it was failure number one for his family. Sigurd could only wish that Herr Hadrid Thorsen, second in command to the *Reichskommissar* for Norway, had shown a little more foresight.

Sigurd had the photos digitally enhanced, but there were items piled on top of each other, making them hard to identify. The hilt of King Olaf's sword stood apart, as well as a chalice and a crude box.

The value of the gold for the metal alone was in

the tens of millions and would be paid back to the SQN's coffers once the gold had been recovered. Then, finally, the Thorsen debt would be repaid.

And while repayment was critical, the gold would never be sold. Sigurd couldn't wait to touch the treasure, sort through it and find that which would bring him to the Table of Three.

The music swelled through the mini earphones, increasing his anticipation. Then it ended and, as always, he felt the rush of power over fate continue on through him. He pulled out the earbuds and closed his eyes to let the imagery of being one of the top three play in his head.

Leaves rustled.

He opened his eyes.

Catherine stood at the edge of the copse, stunning as the outline of her lithe body under her sheer gown was silhouetted by the sun.

All of that was lost by the mere fact that she stood there. Had there been something positive to report, his lieutenant would be standing before him. Instead, they'd sent Catherine to soften his anger.

Something had gone seriously wrong. And he had the sickening feeling whatever happened would have to be reported to Number One.

Catherine smiled at him, a soft curve of her lips, even as her eyes held a hint of shadow. She knew there was a big problem ahead for him to solve.

Sigurd stuffed the photos back in his leather

folio and headed to the house without a word to her. He heard her soft footfalls as she followed him, and once inside the house, she left him to do what needed to be done.

His lieutenant and two of his troops were already assembled in the library.

He listened to the report, holding back his frustration. It was worse than he thought, but he felt the bungled operation didn't lead back to him—the only saving grace.

The SineQuaNon recruit who pulled the trigger and who'd been in charge of photographing Mr. and Mrs. Hunter's movements had vanished, apparently knowing he'd screwed up and had been a bad shot to boot, hitting the old man.

Who was the victim? And who were the two other people with the Hunters? And why did one have a gun? Was he a bodyguard?

Did that mean his partners no longer trusted him? Sigurd thought quickly and realized that wasn't an issue. He could quickly muster SineQuaNon troops who would outnumber any aboard the *Brizo*.

Sigurd sent his lieutenant back to the cathedral to see what was in the tangle of bushes and the remaining two men in his command on a search to find the deserter and get the answers Sigurd needed. Then they'd get rid of the man.

Since more information would soon be coming, Sigurd decided to postpone his report. Hopefully the additional information would be good enough to offset the incredible blunder of these new recruits.

In fact, he decided, it wasn't his blunder at all, it was the training back at the compound that had caused this.

That was what he'd stress in his report. And when he sat at the table of three, he'd make his recommendations to change the training.

Chapter Fifteen

When Hermann first arrived in Trondheim, he located two safe houses that could be used as a last resort. They were located close to the ship and hidden in plain sight, busy with people, with an easy escape time and route. Now that the SineQuaNon was indeed part of this quest, he knew his gut had been right.

Hermann was grateful that Tori and Reid readily agreed with his plan for them to stay on the *Brizo* with the idea that if needed, their foursome—including him and Abby—would be an additional force of power with Captain Andrews's men.

But when it came to convincing Magnus to stay hidden on the ship, Hermann had to be harshly stark in his description of what he meant when he'd said the SineQuaNon wouldn't let up until they had both him and the medallion.

Magnus blanched at the graphic description of what would happen to him once he was found without the small gold disk. They wouldn't kill him for they needed him to be the conduit of the medallion's force. But getting the information about where he'd hidden the medallion would hurt.

Then Hermann relented and they'd talked, engineer to engineer, straight talk without the graphic context. Facts.

After which Magnus agreed to stay on the boat and out of sight. There were plenty of berths on the ship, and he chose one on a lower deck near the bow, out of the way of traffic.

Captain Andrews sent a couple of his men to pick up the items from the hotel on the lists Tori, Reid and Magnus had hastily penned. Magnus was going to be MIA at work, so he would lose his room. He wanted all his notes on the genealogical research he'd done, along with his few bits of clothing and personal items. And his computer.

Hermann had promised to replace anything he needed but didn't retrieve.

Tori and Reid, on the other hand, agreed with Hermann that they needed to keep a sense of presence at the hotel as a red herring if needed. But until it was appropriate that they be seen, they would stay in their stateroom near Hermann's and Abby's.

The boat was getting crowded with the extra crew and passengers, and there was at least one more they'd have to bring aboard: Sigurd Thorsen.

But at the moment, Hermann was alone with Abby in the ship's mess. He sipped the coffee she placed in front of him before she returned to her spot near the coffee urn, her back toward him.

The afternoon sun from the skylight above

kissed the auburn highlights in her hair, and he ached to run the silky strands between his fingers. To smell the light lemon fragrance of her shampoo. She moved as if to turn toward him, then thought better as her shoulders slumped. Abby was still fighting her demon, and he despised that it was stronger than her love for him.

He'd not wanted to bring this up until the job was over, but the stakes had changed; they were fighting on two fronts, the elements and evil. He needed her to be vigilant and think twice before doing anything that would increase their jeopardy.

"Liebchen," he said softly.

She turned to face him.

He rose and took her hand, leading her back to the table. "Please," he said, not letting loose, feeling her fingers try and pull from his. "Sit."

She did, and still he held onto her hand. "I love you, you are my soul . . . "

Tears flooded her eyes, but instead of gathering her to him and ignoring the menace that threatened them both, he had to continue. "I thought I could keep you safe, but I realize you won't let me. Nor can I watch you destroy yourself by the risks you take to capture whatever illusive thing you need that is always out of reach. Only you can fight that demon and win or give in and . . . lose."

He held her gaze, hoping she got what he was telling her. Her eyes gave no hint, but she bit her lip, controlling its slight tremor.

"I can tell you the people we are up against won't hesitate to hurt you, Tori, or Reid. I beg of you, for the duration of this battle, please think of them before you make a rash move that puts them at risk as well as yourself."

"And they'll hurt you," she whispered.

Hermann lifted a shoulder, trying to minimize her focus on him.

"And you," she said again, gripping his hand harder.

He nodded once.

Hermann figured, using his stoic German side, that he could stop searching for the world's hidden objects and would find a way to be content with an engineering life and Abby at his side. But his love? Would she be happy?

He doubted it.

The air between them grew thick with words he needed to hear, that needed to be said, but that didn't come. Nor did he really expect them. Her fervent declaration to Magnus just minutes ago about the thrill of the hunt came straight from her heart.

A knock sounded at the galley door. "Herr Weiss, we've got a ping."

Abby pulled her hand from his before Captain Andrews entered the galley. Hermann wanted to hold it tight, make her realize that what they had was far more important than the need pushing her to take life-endangering risks, especially now. But their moment was over.

"Sir, the AUV has found an object that appears to be a plane."

***

In the dimly lit radar room of the *Brizo*, Abby wanted to reach out to Hermann, to feel his pulse race with the same wonder of discovery that filled her. But the tenseness in his shoulders and the whiteness of his fingers gripping the back of the crewman's chair in front of the AUV's tracking monitor stopped her.

Until he met her gaze. She saw the same excitement she felt in her very soul.

How could he ask her to stop being who she was? *He's not, silly goose. He's asking you to think before you jump too high and fall too deep. To consider those around you.* And though he didn't come out and say it, Hermann meant not simply for the rest of this quest, but to make the decision that would keep them together.

Abby had Tori back in her life, along with Reid. She also had a man who loved her with his entire being, yet she chafed at the restrictions he asked of her. Her parents hadn't let leaving two children at home with their trusted mentor Alfred stop them; they'd gone on to risk life and limb on dangerous finds. And then they'd died in their element.

Now you're grasping at half truths, Abby girl. They died in an airplane crash coming home to you and Tori on your thirteenth birthday. Tori blamed herself for their deaths, which led to her solitary life on the train, and you're acting out their reality . . . leading you to what? An empty existence? A shriveled old lady reliving her heyday, but alone? Assuming I make it to old age?

"What's up? We got your text," Reid said, stepping into the radar room after Tori.

Abby noted his arm went around her sister as she stood beside him, and she tucked away her envy, knowing all she had to do was as Hermann suggested and she too would be in same halo of a lover's touch.

"We've got sonar images," the captain said. "We're holding the AUV at the same point where we first found it, but I want a better angle. Move one degree port, down five degrees, then hold." He directed his sonar man to move the AUV to another position. "Okay, look up at the overhead monitors."

Abby heard the excitement in the captain's voice. He was more dramatic than she'd thought, more adept at keeping the suspense high. But then, he was Scottish.

The black screens instantly came to life with a golden-colored image.

"This is a photograph?" Tori asked.

"Lassie, it's live sonar. It's not static. We can move the AUV and get other angles."

Abby agreed with Tori's surprise. Totally amazing. Her stomach fluttered, not only with excitement of this moment, but the harsh knowledge that men had died in that wreck. As her parents had died in theirs.

There had been a search for the Carswell's plane, but nothing was found. GPS hadn't been invented yet. Neither had this amazing technology.

Wrapping her hands around her middle, Abby focused on the clear but eerie image of a broken plane lying on the bottom of the fjord. The detail the sonar gave was incredible. The massive center engine mounted behind the cockpit looked intact. However, the twin tail of the float plane had broken off and was lying on the silty bottom at nearly a right angle to the fuselage. The wings with the two additional engines had also broken off but stayed in place.

"Can't quite believe we found the ugly sonuvabitch. A BV138. The Sea Dragon was its nickname, or "the flying clog," Reid said. "It's appropriate."

"Look at those rectangular objects scattered around the sides and back of the plane. Do you think they are the crates holding the gold?" Abby whispered. Not because she didn't want anyone to hear, but because with every discovery the awe of actually finding the unfindable stole her breath. Without thinking, she grabbed Hermann's arm and felt his hand cover hers. Like he had before their dive only three days ago.

"Can we see any more detail of the crates with the AUV's sonar?" Reid pointed to the one of the rectangular mounds.

"Very little, sir. The water's turbidity and the depth would disperse the lights from the AUV. It's time to deploy the ROV," Captain Andrews said.

"Which means Sigurd will demand to be here. We can explain away your presence on board," Abby said, turning to Reid and Tori. "But not Magnus's."

"Ja, I agree."

"But we don't know if Sigurd is aware of who Magnus is yet," Tori said. "And he's got no place else to be."

"Speaking of the man, where is he?"

"In the crew quarters," Reid said. "He didn't want to come in and be in the way."

"I don't understand why he can't just stay there," Tori said. "We can take him food or whatever."

"Lassie, I suppose he could, but we will be out at sea for days. The ROV has to be tethered to the *Brizo* to do its work. While Jack here," Captain Andrews patted the crewman's shoulder, "will operate the vehicle and manipulator arm."

"I think I have an idea," Hermann said.

Chapter Sixteen

Hermann's idea was just the kind of activity Reid loved to plan. And the pressure was on, because Reid knew Hermann was correct when he said they had to do it all before Sigurd boarded the *Brizo* or lose their opportunity.

First they had to get Magnus off the boat unseen, as they were sure they were being watched.

Removing him from the boat covertly wouldn't be a difficult task. Reid noticed that Captain Andrews had a large provisions container that was used daily and could be hauled off without suspicion, especially since the ship was undergoing other preparations for leaving port. It was busy topside.

The rest of the plan was a matter of timing, phone calls and gadgets.

At the moment Reid was waiting for some of said gadgets Hermann thought would be useful. Unable to sit for another minute, he leaned against the wall of the mess, his arms around Tori, whom he'd pulled against his chest.

Abby was ready for this escapade. Tori he

wasn't so sure of, and Magnus looked green as he paced the mess, then stopped to stare at the container that was going to be his way off the ship. Then he paced again.

"I can do this with Abby. You don't have to come along," Reid whispered against her hair.

She shook her head slightly. "You're not going anywhere without me, besides—"

At that moment, Hermann returned from wherever he kept his stash of gear on the ship. Reid let go of Tori but didn't share her blush at being caught in a clinch.

Hermann set four pairs of high tech glasses on the table along with three small canvas bags. "Google glasses?" Reid asked, picking up one pair to inspect.

"Weiss glasses," Hermann answered with a slight grin. "If you press this,"—he pointed to a minute, screw-like button on the side of the binoculars—"it will feed whatever you see to each of us. There is an infrared mode button next to that, and on the other side is the Internet connection I'll use to communicate with you. The mic is voice activated and built in. It's very sensitive, so it will pick up a whisper, but it's short range, so I'll text my communications and they'll appear on the screen. Abby, what you need is in the green bag. Magnus gets the gray and Reid the black. Are you ready?"

Reid noticed Hermann wasn't looking at him when he asked the question. So he was concerned as well about Tori's readiness for all this.

"You guys quit coddling me. I'll be fine. I've already been shot at, and remember, I can outrun both of you."

Magnus folded his lanky frame into the tight plastic provisions crate. Abby handed him the three small bags. She lowered the lid and they waited until they heard Magnus's rap on the container's top. Then Hermann signaled and four crew members crowded into the galley, hefted the crate and carried it to the fan deck to be loaded into the Zodiac.

"Okay, Abby, you're on," Reid said, feeling a bit like a movie director. "Remember, Hermann will join you in a few minutes."

She straightened her costume, a short, beaded party dress, grabbed her prop—two glasses of wine—and headed topside. They'd look like a couple toasting the midnight sun.

Hermann glanced at his watch. "Time for me to go." Before he left, he bussed Tori lightly on the cheek. "Be safe."

Now it was just him and Tori. "Okay, let's give them a couple of minutes, then it's show time," Reid said.

"You like this, don't you?"

"Yes, I do, but I'll give it all up if it's something you don't want to be a part of."

"I don't really like that we can die doing this, but I do like the hunt and the thrill of finding something lost. Maybe I have more of Abby inside me than I thought."

"Darlin', you're twins." He mock-grimaced when she punched his arm. "I wish Abby had more of you inside her. She's still charging into situations full tilt, and I think it's bugging Hermann."

"Yeah, I saw the look too. Maybe I can talk to her after this is over."

They heard the Zodiac's engine rev, then fade as it left the boat. Their cue.

It was past 10 p.m. and the sun still hung slightly above the horizon, lighting everything. This was the one drawback to Reid's part of the plan, but there wasn't any other possibility as the midnight sun lasted way into the wee hours of the morning.

Up on the *Brizo's* deck, Abby made a show of drinking the last of her wine and kissing Hermann. Reid appeared with Tori, then the trio left Hermann and headed down the gangplank and along the dock to the Clarion Hotel. Abby stopped and turned, waving to Hermann, who remained standing on the deck, watching them go. They'd staged this to look like an innocent night out, so that whoever was watching them would assume nothing more was happening. And they were being watched. The shooting at the cathedral made that clear.

Reid and Hermann decided that the risk of being seen was tempered by being in crowded places, and the dock area was filled with Rockheim

Museum goers. In fact, people thronged the entire area up to and past the hotel.

Nevertheless, they'd placed two crew members at the hotel, one in the lobby and one on the fifth floor near their room. The trio passed the *Brizo* crew member in the hotel lobby eating a snack. Reid caught his eye and the man nodded. So far so good, all the way to their room.

Once there, Tori and Reid quickly changed into dressy, doing-the-town clothes, and Tori packed a set of dark clothing for each of them in her large traveling purse. Not quite the right accessory for evening wear, but it was better than a backpack. Then Tori swiftly packed their small carry-on bag and left it on the bed.

"Good thing we're still the same size," Abby said and pulled Tori aside. "Are you sure you're ready for this? I don't want to push you into something you don't want to do."

"I'm a little nervous, naturally. But I think I'm going to be fine. And Reid's worried too, naturally."

"*Naturally*, but he's still doing this."

"He'd quit if I asked him to."

"Will you?"

"No, I don't think so. What about you? You're edgy tonight."

"I'm fine."

Reid pretended he couldn't hear them, but Abby was definitely edgy. Her performance on the deck as half the loving couple looked strained. What the hell was going on with her and Hermann?

"Ready?" At their nods, Reid knocked loudly on their room door and received a knock back from the watching crewman. They were clear to go.

Before the elevator reached the lobby, Reid had the twins flank him, hooking their arms through his. Laughing as the door slid open, they strolled through the lobby of the hotel. Reid basked in the envious glances he got from the males in the room. "You both are making the men green with envy," he whispered, earning another laugh. They strolled through the lobby, and he knew he had the best of the best on his arms.

They passed the crewman now outside reading a tourist pamphlet. Again another quick nod, then the man grinned seeing Abby and Tori dolled up and on Reid's arm. He shared the smile, feeling pretty darn lucky.

He chose a random taxi from the queue at the hotel's entrance and asked to be dropped off at the Rica Nidelven Hotel, which was conveniently located on the Nidelva River and had its own docks.

Giving the driver a good tip for such a short journey made without complaint, Reid again flanked himself with the twins and entered the hotel's lobby. They found the restrooms on the lobby level. He changed into khaki cargo pants and a green T-shirt that unfortunately had a white logo dead center, so he turned it inside out.

Meeting the girls near the door, he laughed. They both had on khaki pants and green long-sleeved T-shirts and wore their hair in a topknot. Totally twins. Or maybe, including him, triplets by what they wore.

As they'd decided earlier, Tori and Abby left the hotel together and Reid followed them, rendezvousing behind the hotel on the third pier, where the *Brizo's* Zodiac was now moored.

The two crewmen that had piloted it away from the *Brizo* with Magnus in the crate waited for them on the pier with the crate between. Just then Reid's phone vibrated and he checked the text from Hermann. *Safe at home.* He showed it to Abby and Tori. Magnus was secure in the safe house.

"I'm not expecting us to need more than three hours, but if it's longer than four, you know to contact Herr Weiss."

The two crewmen nodded.

Tori pulled their evening clothes from her large traveling bag, and Reid handed her his bundle. The purse went into the crate with the clothes neatly laid on top.

Reid helped Tori and Abby into the boat, and the crewmen cast off the lines.

They weren't in a hurry as Hermann wouldn't call Sigurd until they were in place. Nor did they want to bring attention to themselves on the river, so Reid kept the powerful motor throttled down. They looked like tourists.

Tori craned her neck, looking at all the poling houses flanking the banks of the river. "I love the bright oranges, reds, forest greens, and even the whites. Most have been carefully restored. I bet that cost a fortune."

He was grateful she looked relaxed on the water, even excited and engaged in her foreign surroundings. He'd worried that even motoring up the broad river would be too much for her.

She glanced at him and their gazes held. Reid realized it was as she'd said in Hawaii. They were together and that made all the difference in how one approached and conquered fear.

He cruised under the bridge near Sigurd's house and cut the boat's motor as they approached their target.

***

Reid beached the boat on the river bank under the broad, concealing branches of a tree about one hundred yards down from Sigurd's house. Abby snagged her equipment from the green duffel bag Hermann had prepared, and Reid grabbed the black one. He pulled out the "Weiss Glasses," handing them to Tori and Abby and slipping on a pair himself.

"Go into share mode, now." Reid pushed the little button on the glasses. He could see superimposed images of what Tori and Abby were seeing. He moved away from them. "I'm connected, are you?" he whispered.

"Roger," Abby said and Tori echoed.

Got you all as well. Hermann's message flashed up on one edge of the lens. He could see what they saw, communicate via text but not hear them.

Quickly stuffing the rest of the tools he needed into his cargo pants pockets, Reid zipped the bag and threw it over his shoulder. “Okay then, let's go.”

Abby moved toward the bushes that ran along the south property line. He and Tori darted through the many trees along the bank, giving them enough cover from the midnight sun to move easily within the shadows until they got to the copse and rune stone.

Reid placed the duffel on one of the stone slab benches, then he and Tori darted to the line of trees that ran along the north side of Sigurd's house.

The trees gave way to bushes and there they stopped.

“In place,” Reid said softly.

“Same here,” Abby responded.

Reid really liked these new tools. Hermann had upped the game with these glasses. It was far easier than fumbling with phones or earpieces and mics. And being able to see what your fellow conspirators saw was incredibly helpful.

All remained quiet. The image he was getting from Abby's glasses was a clear shot of the front of the house. Minutes later, he watched as several of the staff they'd seen during their dinner with Sigurd exited the front door.

“I counted seven,” Tori whispered.

“Yep, I got that too. That was the same number as the staff we saw, plus the chef and the housekeeper." Reid kept his voice to a whisper as well.

"How do you know that?"

"It's a good habit to know your position and your odds. There had to be a chef, and I'm guessing the one in the checkered pants is him, and the older lady? I'm guessing she's the housekeeper or whatever they call them here."

"I'm impressed. I didn't even realize you were keeping count. Do you count cards as well?"

"No, that's cheating."

Tori's gentle laugh washed over him, broken by Abby's whispered snort. A text from Hermann ran across his glasses. *Just made the call.* "Did you all get that?"

"Yes. I'm expecting Sigurd to come out any minute," Abby said.

They didn't have to wait long.

Sigurd exited the house carrying a small bag, flanked by two men wearing larger duffel bags on their backs. Catherine stood framed in the doorway, backlit by the lights in the house. The men mounted motorcycles as Sigurd got into his Mercedes. Abby was moving her head so the glasses would track their movement. The image was clear. They split at the driveway with Sigurd heading to the *Brizo* and the two men going the opposite way.

Interesting, Reid thought. They weren't the bodyguards he'd expected, who would have stay glued to Sigurd. So what were they and where were they headed?

Catherine closed the door, and one by one lights turned off until the house was dark. “Abby, switch to infrared.” The image changed and it was as he'd guessed, tiny red laser beams crisscrossed each window and the door at the front of the house. “Okay, got it. Back to shared view.”

And again he saw the normal view of the front of the house.

He switched his glasses to infrared and saw all the windows and doors along the back of house were also covered with those red crisscrossing lines.

Now was the time to check out his theory. Hopefully nothing was crisscrossing that impossibly small opening.

Reid turned to Tori. “Ready?” He'd wanted her to stay back in the trees, but she nixed that idea without hesitation.

She nodded.

“Okay, Abby, do your magic.”

The street lamps and the houses around 3 Sverres Gate went dark.

The midnight sun made this next step the most difficult. It was light enough to look out a window and see someone moving in the gardens. Thus the green shirt and cargo pants. But what Reid was counting on was the gap of a few seconds between the outage and what he would expect to happen: Sigurd's independent power source would kick on.

During those seconds the surveillance cameras

he'd noted during their dinner there would be out of commission and give them time to use the low angle of the sun. It would create shadows deep enough for them to move from the concealment of the trees to the bushes that hid what he hoped would be their way into the house.

They sprinted.

Tori got there first and grabbed him, pulling him into the bushes near the house. He landed with a grunt just as the telltale red light from the cameras blinked on. Quickly they ducked behind the bushes near the house.

From the duffel he pulled a small camp shovel and dug into the hard soil, quickly removing just enough dirt to reveal the small window pane of old and thick warped glass set into the foundation of the house. Eureka, it was free of those nasty crisscrossing red lines.

For the same reason he'd counted the staff, Reid had spent time on the Internet and found pictures from the 1940s of this mansion, and he'd seen the window. Now bushes and decades of soil hid it from view, and he was sure nobody knew of its existence.

The odds were now in their favor.

Cutting a small hole in the window with a diamond-tipped glass cutter, Reid turned on the small device Hermann had given him and pushed it through the hole. It didn't make a sound or create any light, but the high-energy pulse it emitted was supposed to disrupt the laser beams. Reid flipped his lens to infrared and looked up. “Come on, come on, work,” he whispered.

“Got it,” Tori whispered. Sure enough the laser crisscrossing the windows above him faded, then disappeared.

“Abby, we're going in, start the countdown.”

He turned to Tori. “Don't forget plan B, because I think we're going to need it.” After he kissed her forehead, Reid quickly picked the lock on the door at the back of the house he'd noticed the servers using during the dinner party. He slipped in first, followed by Tori.

Easing through the dark kitchen, using a red-filtered flashlight, they moved into the hall. No sign of Catherine. Reid prayed the hinges wouldn't creak when he opened the library door.

Silence.

He played the light over the walls to the desk. There sat Catherine.

With a gun pointed at them.

***

Catherine held a semi-automatic with a suppressor attached. Nobody would hear a thing if he and Tori were shot.

“I know you're wondering. Yes, I do know how to use this,” Catherine said, her voice deadly calm. “If you turn off your light, thinking you'll blind me by the darkness, I can guarantee my bullet will find your woman.”

Crap. Plan B.

Reid shrugged. “Okay. Then answer me one

question before you call the police. Why do you stay with him? You're just a pawn, a toy. A perk."

That did it, the gun wavered just enough.

He pushed the button on his flashlight and the room went dark.

He heard the soft cough of the gun and prayed Tori had moved as they'd planned. Her extraordinary speed was their saving grace.

In a second he was behind Catherine, his hands on either side of her head, ready to twist hard and break her neck if she didn't behave.

Tori turned on her flashlight, took the gun from Catherine's fingers and tucked it in the back of her waistband.

"I have two questions for you. Your answers decide your fate. You want to leave this life, don't you? Be free, go your own way? Not be a trophy. Even if you're a well-kept one, you're still a prisoner."

"Mr. Hunter, why do you think I'm not here of my own free will?"

"The way you're treated," Tori answered for Reid.

Reid hadn't expected Catherine's question, but he appreciated Tori's answer. It was to the point. "The clock is ticking—"

"For both of us."

Damn she was a hard cookie. Well then, he'd play hardball, too. "You get one try, then your release will be permanent. Like dead. Question number one: which bookcase hides the entrance to

Herr Thorsen's private office? And question number two, what is the password to his computer?"

"It doesn't matter what you do to me, I can't leave. I have no money to escape and if I did, I can't buy a new identity, and if I give you the answers you want, I'll be dead as soon as Sigurd returns. So go ahead and twist now, and I'll be free."

Bingo, he got to her. "You can leave. There is a black bag with money stashed by the rune stone." Reid nodded in the direction of the garden. "Inside the bag there is a phone with two numbers programmed in. Captain Andrews on the *Brizo*, and the number of a man who will get you away and give you a new identity. Alfred's good, really good. And lastly, taped to the phone is the address of a safe house. I promise you it's all legit."

"Why would you do this?"

"Because nobody should be the chattel of someone else," Tori said. "And you are just that."

"It's hard to believe you're kind just because–"

"Believe it or not, it's true," Tori said softly.

"Tick tock," Reid said, worried that too much time was slipping past them. The electrical impulse scrambler he'd tossed in the little window had a limited lifespan. And sooner rather than later, the utility company would be coming out to check on the neighborhood outage Abby created with another of Hermann's gadgets.

The seconds ticked by. Sweat was beginning to drip between his shoulder blades. Despite his threats, Reid wouldn't kill her. But he wasn't at all sure they could carry her out if he incapacitated her. And then what? Keep her prisoner on the *Brizo*? Not with Sigurd there.

And Reid couldn't leave her here. Damn, she needed to capitulate and give them what they needed. Take the freedom they offered her.

"As you thought, his office is behind us. See the small vase on the shelf. It's old school," she said with a slight smile. "Pull it and the door opens."

Reid watched Tori carefully, still keeping his hands on Catherine's head, worried that a trap might activate as the vase was pulled back.

A narrow section of the bookcase swung open. Pulling it open wider, Tori slipped in. "Got the computer," she called.

"Now for the password."

"I have no idea, but take the computer," Catherine said. "There are two flash drives in the bottom compartment of the left drawer. Only Sigurd and I know about them. He'll know eventually that the house was broken into, but if the flash drives and computer are gone along with me, he'll think I've taken them and that will give you more time."

"And why would you do that?"

"Repayment. If the bag doesn't have all you've offered, I can contact Sigurd and tell him I was your captive when you broke in."

Reid heard Tori opening a drawer in the office, some clunking of wood together, and then the drawer shutting.

"Okay, got the flash drives. And Reid, come in here. Bring Catherine with you."

"Keep your hands at your side," he ordered. "Move."

Reid entered after Catherine, keeping his gaze on her hands. Tori handed him the gun, and he kept it trained on the woman.

The room was narrow, filled by an ornate antique desk. Neatly tacked up on the wall in front of the desk were enlargements of the photos Sigurd had given Hermann and Abby and they in turn had given Reid and Tori.

These weren't burned and damaged as the ones Sigurd had shown them and said he found in his father's possessions. Reid figured Sigurd damaged them to set the hook deeper in Hermann and Abby.

The photographs of the treasure circled a full-sized poster of a couple holding a baby girl.

"What do you think, early 1940s?"

Tori looked closer. "By the clothes, yes."

"That's what Sigurd believed as well," Catherine said.

The woman, seated in the same chair that still graced the library in this house, wore a flowing evening gown of organza topped with white or cream lace. On the upper left bodice she wore the same medallion that was now hidden in Magnus's leather photo frame. She held a baby dressed in what looked like a Christening gown.

Standing behind the woman was a man that looked vaguely like Magnus. He was dressed in the formal clothes of the period.

"I'm betting the baby is Brigitte."

Now we have proof. Sigurd is SineQuaNon. Hermann's text flashed on all three lenses.

"Sigurd is SineQuaNon." Reid looked at Catherine. "Right?"

"Yes."

"And how many people know about this room?"

"Two, Sigurd and me."

"Time—your scrambler is about done," Abby said.

***

Reid snatched the photo of Magnus's great grandparents with baby Brigitte from the wall, then had Catherine walk in front of him, followed by Tori, moving single file to the kitchen door. Now he had to decide whether or not to believe Catherine. She could grab the bag, keep the money, ditch the phone and still report them to Sigurd. Additionally, those two men who left on the motorcycles worried him. But Hermann had more men aboard the ship, and he and Captain Andrews were on the alert for any odd moves Sigurd might make.

"Make the right choice," he warned Catherine. "This is your way out. This or a bullet." He didn't want to hurt her. Catherine was, as Tori said, chattel to Sigurd, thus basically a slave to the

SineQuaNon. He'd seen it before in nearly every dark organization from the Chinese Triad to the Russian Mob.

Catherine spun and ran across the yard, straight toward the copse and the rune stone, obviously not worried about being seen. And why should she? She supposedly belonged here.

“Okay, right decision, so far,” he murmured. “Abby, we're out.”

Reid grabbed Tori's hand and ran hard toward the edge of the trees. He glanced in the direction of the rune stone, noting the bag was gone, as was Catherine. Reaching the banks of the Nidelva, Reid turned his glasses to infrared one more time and saw the laser lines now crossing all the windows.

They'd made it with seconds to spare.

Abby met them at the boat.

“That was close—a utility van was just coming down the street. It sounded like Catherine made the right choice. Even helped you with the flash drives.”

Reid nodded. “It will be interesting to see what's on those.” He guided the inflatable boat up the river, staying as close as possible to the deepening shadows. No sense in being careless now.

“To think Cindy Jones...Ødegård worked several jobs to make ends meet when all that wealth was sitting there,” Tori said.

“Then you're thinking the same thing. The house Sigurd lives in should be Magnus's,” Reid said.

"I wonder if he'll ever get to live there. The SineQuaNon wants him. And until that's over—"

"Over? It's a centuries-old society. I don't know if it'll ever be destroyed, Abby," Reid said. "It's like cutting heads off a hydra—more spring forth."

"That's a lovely thought."

Reid smiled at her tart reply.

Slipping into the mooring spot behind the Hotel Nidelva, where the crewmen still waited, they changed back into their fancy clothes in the shadows of the pier as the crew stood guard, backs turned.

The crewmen loaded the now-empty crate with provisions a van had delivered earlier. They hefted it into the Zodiac and took off.

Reid led the way to the street and hailed a taxi.

They reached the Clarion hotel and again Reid tipped the driver generously for the short trip.

One more time Reid had Tori and Abby flank him, and together they entered the lobby.

The crew member who'd kept lobby watch was again at the bar, chatting with a few women. He rubbed his lip, hiding the fact he was talking into a subvocal microphone to Captain Andrews.

Reid stopped close to him and bent down to tie his shoe, watching him from the corner of his eyes.

The yawn came. All was safe on the *Brizo*.

Deliberately, he bumped against the man.

"Oh, sorry," he said.

"No harm done," was the reply.

Reid knew the claim ticket was in his pocket. He and the twins headed to the concierge desk and presented the stub for the small carry-on bag Tori had packed earlier, which the crewman monitoring the hallway had retrieved and stored.

With the bag in hand, they headed down the pier and to the ship.

Chapter Seventeen

After Abby, Tori and Reid were back aboard, Captain Andrews left port and headed the *Brizo* to the position where the AUV had located the downed plane.

At first light, they'd launched the ROV, and it was now painstakingly plotting the wreck.

Already, Hermann had his fill of Sigurd, who continually paced the small sonar room, basically being a nuisance.

"Move it left more," Sigurd said.

Hermann watched as the ROV stayed its course, photographing everything before it started any actual retrieval operations.

"I said—"

"Sir," Jack spoke the word with as little sincerity as he could get away with, "the grid has to be followed and plotted. Those are the captain's instructions."

Hermann swallowed his smile at Jack's reply and kept his posture relaxed as Sigurd moved directly in front of him, stopping inches from his face. He met Sigurd's narrowed eyes with a steady gaze of his own.

"Aren't you the captain's employer—"

Hermann held up a hand, interrupting his tirade. "While aboard the *Brizo*, Captain Andrews has full command of the ship, her operations and crew," he said with, he hoped, enough emphasis to end the string of demands the man had made since the boat left the dock before daylight.

From the moment Sigurd boarded the ship, he'd whined about his accommodations being a deck below the suites the master crew occupied, saying pointedly, "None of this would be happening if it weren't for me."

And when he'd had to wait for the trio of faux party-goers to return before the *Brizo* could leave port, he stood at the gangplank, hands on his hips. "So glad you had time to drink and dance. Now we can finally get underway," he sneered.

"Well, at least you don't have to wait longer. We stopped by the hotel to pack," Reid had said as Tori held up the small suitcase.

So far their plan had worked flawlessly. But Hermann knew that luck could change in a heartbeat, now that they were certain whom they were dealing with. The SineQuaNon was a society known for their brutality and cunning. Hermann had everyone on full alert.

Sigurd's phone rang and he stepped out of the room to take the call.

Hermann met Jack's gaze with a smile. "Nice work."

"Thanks, sir."

When Sigurd stepped back into the sonar room, tension radiated off him. He drummed his fingers on the doorframe and kept clenching his jaw. His eyes glittered with suppressed fury as he glanced at Hermann.

Hermann would bet his bottle of Remy Martin Louis XIII cognac that Sigurd just found out Catherine had vanished.

Captain Andrews hadn't yet received Catherine's phone call, and Hermann hadn't heard from Alfred in days, knowing the man would be in touch once Catherine called him. But at the moment, her lack of communication didn't worry him as he understood she had to feel safe before taking any further actions. What she'd done already by leaving Sigurd and the SineQuaNon was a bold step.

"Are we closer to being done?" Sigurd's voice vibrated with fury.

Hermann kept him within his peripheral vision as a precaution, having seen in at least one prior instance that Sigurd's temper manifested itself physically when his laptop had been the recipient of his anger back in Oregon.

Hermann didn't want him smashing the delicate equipment in the sonar room or taking a swipe at the crew.

"Yes, sir, we are. I've completed the plotting and sent it to the printer," Jack said.

At that moment Captain Andrews entered the

small sonar room with a roll of paper tucked under his arm. "It'll be easier to see the print spread out on the larger table in the mess," he said, cupping the end of the roll with his hand as Sigurd reached for it. "Jack, take a break for a while. You've been at it for hours."

"Aye, sir. Some fresh air will be good." Jack stood and stretched.

Hermann saw him glance at Sigurd as he left the room, knowing full well that Jack meant fresh air was anywhere away from the difficult man.

"After you." Hermann gestured his antsy partner toward the door, then followed along with Andrews to the mess.

Abby was seated at the table talking casually to Reid and Tori, looking unconcerned, even a bit bored by the wait. They were all playing their parts well, since both Hermann and the captain knew everyone was on high alert.

Andrews unrolled the chart on the mess table. Then he placed photographs from the ROV to correspond with the sonar images.

The captain pointed to what appeared to be lumps under a buildup of silt.

"The ROV captured these in more detail. I believe these to be the crates. But from the damage to the tail booms, and the fact that these are more bump- than box-shaped, I'd guess none of the crates remained intact—"

"Meaning we can't get to the gold?" Sigurd stabbed his finger on the chart.

"No, sir, it means that it might take more work and more time. We're ready to engage the manipulator arm. We're above here now," the captain pointed to what looked like a jumble of mounds.

"Then let's get started," Sigurd said.

Andrews turned to Hermann, who nodded.

"Then I'll leave you and get Jack back to his station." The captain left the mess, leaving the chart on the table for them to study.

"Sigurd, I feel I must remind you that Captain Andrews will not take orders from anyone but me."

Sigurd flushed and stared at them, his fists clenching spasmodically. Then he stalked from the mess.

"Poor Jack, he didn't get much of a break from Sigurd. I was going to tell our partner"—Hermann emphasized the last word—"that there is a video feed from the sonar room to the TV here." He turned on the flat screen mounted on the wall.

"Glad you didn't. He must know by now that his fortress has been penetrated," Reid said.

"And to that point, I had Andrews bring an additional two more men aboard last night, ostensibly as crew to help with the ROV. Sigurd did get a call while we were in the sonar room and came back very agitated."

Captain Andrews's voice came through the TV's speakers. "Okay, Jack, easy. Let's see what's under there."

They turned their attention to the screen and

watched as the manipulator claw moved downward. “God, it's even in color. The lights are strong enough for us to see everything,” Tori said, her voice tight with excitement.

Then the claw penetrated the silt. The water clouded immediately, obscuring the camera's eye.

Hermann noticed Abby's slight shudder. She must be recalling their dive when the same thing happened to her.

He'd been concerned she might investigate something that compelled her to leave the safety of the ledge, so had planted a beacon in her dry suit as he'd zipped her up. It was the only thing that saved her. He hadn't told her he'd done so, because he knew she'd resent his overprotectiveness, just as he knew she wasn't happy being in the middle on the shot line during their dive.

This time she'd been lucky. But, given her soul-deep need to play God and take on a challenge despite the odds, he might not always have the chance to protect her.

“I don't understand how Jack can see to do anything until the silt clears,” Tori said, standing by the screen, confusion wrinkling her brow.

Hermann pulled himself back to the present and Tori's question.

“He's using the coordinates to place the claw, which is why the mapping of the site was so important, and when he feels something obstructing it, he'll stop until he can either get a visual or Andrews gives him the go-ahead to pull it up," Hermann answered.

"Okay, Jack, easy now," Captain Andrews said. "You should be on it—"

"For God's sake, don't be so cautious—"

"Mr. Thorsen, please," said Andrews, his tone firm, brooking no more interference. "Okay, Jack, see if the claw can find anything to grasp."

"Is the claw that sensitive?" Tori squinted at the TV screen.

"No, Darlin', but the operator is," Reid said, moving so he stood behind Tori, wrapping his arms around her waist and pulling her tight so she rested against his chest.

Hermann smiled at the newlyweds' obvious bliss. It should have been him and Abby as well. Even though he was heartbreakingly frustrated with Abby, he couldn't stand the physical distance between them, and grasped her hand. He felt her glance and met it. A deep sadness underlaid the excitement in her gray eyes. He understood the warring emotions well.

They watched silently as the arm retracted and brought the claw toward the camera. It held a gold bar. The arm moved toward the specimen container box mounted in front of the ROV and carefully placed the bar inside.

"Do you recall gold bars being in the photographs?" Abby asked.

"No, none. But perhaps they were transporting additional items they stole," Hermann said.

"This is going to take too long," Sigurd

complained, his voice made more whiny by the TV speakers.

"I agree," Captain Andrews said.

Hermann smiled as Jack knew exactly what had to be done as the screen showed he directed the manipulator claw to grab a flexible fine-mesh strainer from the side of the container box and scoop it into the silt, bringing it up above the silt cloud that once again bloomed in the water.

The camera zoomed in closer to the mesh and, among the gold bars, something oval-shaped glinted in the ROV's lights.

"That looks like what I'd expect from the pictures," Reid said.

"Another gold bar? Where are the gold pieces?" Sigurd's voice came through the speakers, his tone revealing a man stretched tight.

"I think I better go to the sonar room," Hermann said.

"I'm coming with you," Reid said. "Sooner or later he's going to realize the medallion isn't down there, and he'll go off the deep end."

***

Tori's gaze followed Reid and Hermann out of the mess, then she saw her sister get up and start to follow the men to the sonar room. "Would you come back and sit down, please?"

"I think I should be up there."

"*I* think you're avoiding me, Abigail Carswell. And it's time we have a talk. There is nothing either of us can do at the moment to help the excavation and recovery." Tori didn't want to sound like a bitch, but enough was enough. "Sit."

Abby slid back into the seat.

Tori hadn't actually expected Abby to honor the request, so that was a good start. She just hoped Abby wouldn't pull her old routine of polite avoidance. "What the hell is going on with you and Hermann? It's not icy between you—you still hold hands. It's more of a sadness. I watch him look at you and see love *and* a wall building in his eyes."

Tori hadn't expected the distress that filled her sister's eyes.

Abby turned pale, her lips trembled and she cradled her head on her arms and cried. Deep heaving sobs that shook her shoulders.

Tori slid into the banquette next to Abby and turned her so she could hold her. "What is it?"

"I messed up, again. And Hermann basically . . . " She gulped for air.

"Take your time, Ab." This was going to be far worse than a lover's spat. But she couldn't imagine them breaking up. They were soul mates as much as she and Reid were. They belonged together.

Her twin's nose was running and her eyes were already red and swollen from the torrent of tears she'd apparently pent up for the last few days.

"Hermann thinks I've got a death wish or something close to that. He doesn't . . . no . . . he won't stand by and let me destroy myself, and maybe the rest of us, with what he calls my recklessness."

Wow. This was going to take some careful phrasing. "And do you agree with his . . . assessment that you're being reckless?"

"Do you?"

She should have predicted that Abby would turn the tables on her. Handing her twin a napkin from the rack bolted to the wall below the mess window, Tori watched her sister mop her face as she searched for the right words.

"Yes," Tori blurted.

Abby's hand stilled, and she scooted across the banquette out of Tori's embrace. Raising her chin, Abby smoothed out the wrinkles in the tear-sodden napkin and placed it on the table with great deliberation.

Well, damn! Regardless of her agreement with Hermann's assessment that Abby was being rash, Tori wasn't going to let her rebuild the wall between them they'd broken down the past year.

Tori searched her twin's face, concerned that she wore her polite "I'm listening but that's all" expression.

The only hope Tori had now was that something in her words would hit a nerve. "For a long time I wondered why we became so different after Mom and Dad died. After all, we'd been on the same wave length since we were born. Then it was gone. Poof."

Abby blinked, and Tori saw a shade of detachment leave her eyes.

She forged onward. "Mexico made me realize

that I was living my life with too many limitations. I'd boxed myself in because it felt safer. No connections, no pain. Which was something our Alfred had tried to tell me. Hell, he was even on the brink of moving out to make his point.

"You went in the opposite direction and took all limits off. As if you were saying bring on the pain, the fear, I'm bigger than it. And yes, you scare me with the risks you take. I've stood by, watching and worrying. Maybe someday I won't be able to watch any longer. Hermann, it seems, is at that point now. But you know, Ab, some limits are okay, even a good thing."

Tori ached to embrace her twin, to feel the connection they'd so recently resurrected, when instead Abby reached out and touched her clenched hands. Instantly she felt Abby's energy, but also the fast flutter of panic.

"It's about choices. You get to make the choices, but you have to live with the consequences. Hermann wants you, and I want you to choose us. Selfish, but the choice of love and being loved doesn't have to be confining. Frankly, it's liberating."

***

The *Brizo's* sonar room was stuffy, filled with Sigurd's hot air. Hermann rolled his neck and watched Reid do the same. They shared an exasperated look. They'd spent hours listening to Sigurd complain about the speed of the work and what was being found, as if they had any control over what was down at the bottom of the fjord.

"Sir," Jack said, looking at the Captain. "The retrieval basket—"

"Enough chatter. I want to *see* what has been recovered so far," Sigurd said.

Captain Andrews turned his back to Sigurd. Hermann knew the captain's patience was wearing down and now apparently had worn out.

All of them had been on the alert since the shooting at the cathedral, and now that the snake named Sigurd Thorsen of the SineQuaNon was coiled in plain view, they waited tensely for him to strike. Seeing the treasure might be the moment, but until he had it all and realized the medallion wasn't among the objects, Hermann didn't think Sigurd would make a move.

"You were saying, Jack," Andrews said.

"That the retrieval basket is full." Jack finished his sentence.

Hermann interpreted Andrews's raised eyebrow and nodded. He'd expected Sigurd to demand seeing the recovered items long before now.

"Bring it up, then. I'm sure you could use a break after it's secured."

Even though it would be a minimum of thirty minutes before the ROV surfaced, Sigurd left the sonar room, followed closely by Reid.

Hermann was alone with his thoughts. He'd planned the best he could and now it was a matter of time.

Captain Andrews had divers ready to enter the water when the ROV reached the surface. They'd attach the crane's hooks and cables to the scavenging machine and bring it aboard the *Brizo*.

Hermann made sure all the crew as well as their foursome would be topside and primed for battle if need be. If Sigurd decided this was the time to attack, his backup would have to already be strategically placed.

They weren't the only boat in the fjord. It was summer and diving vessels were around; fishermen and scenic cruises abounded. Any of those could be camouflage for his troops.

This time the midnight sun worked in their favor. This time they would see an attack coming.

From the moment of the shooting at the cemetery, Hermann knew in his gut that there was no way that they could extract themselves from this job. Eventually Sigurd would find out that it was Magnus at the cemetery. That he was the keeper of the medallion. SineQuaNon wouldn't kill him, but the rest of them?

Expendable.

They couldn't be allowed to live, even if they escaped now. As long as Sigurd lived he'd hunt them down. They all knew too much.

Reid had asked Hermann why they shouldn't just kill him and be done. Hermann owed Reid the courtesy of being completely frank as his and Tori's lives were on the line as well.

He was sure that even if they killed Sigurd,

they wouldn't be free of the long tentacles of the SineQuaNon.

Reid had searched his face and then nodded. He wasn't naïve or inexperienced. And Hermann knew Reid would protect Tori to the last.

As one last precaution, Hermann had given Reid the combo to his safe.

Hermann stared at the now blank sonar screen. He should have followed the instinct that had saved him before. Following his gut versus reacting with pride to the gauntlet Sigurd had slapped in his face. The man had taunted him about his father without saying it explicitly. And Hermann had taken the bait.

The minute the SineQuaNon specter had risen, Hermann had tried reaching Alfred Choy. Simple message. "SineQuaNon involved." That was more than twenty-four hours ago. And though he hadn't yet received a reply, he was sure Alfred had received the message. If not, the phone would have shown a green screen, meaning Alfred was in trouble.

Hermann understood Alfred had his own agenda with the society's destruction.

Most of the Chinese man's life had been spent searching out this group. He had compatriots all over the globe trying to find the objects the SineQuaNon wanted, and destroy them before the SineQuaNon could attain them.

The Stone of Heaven in the Yucatan had been one of those. Alfred hadn't wanted Abby to go searching; he'd been working with Dr. Sanchez and they had good solid leads.

Abby did go, and it had been near disaster.

Abby had compounded her sin by not telling Hermann she was attempting the Yucatan hunt. If she had, Hermann thought, he'd have moved heaven and earth to stop her.

But you wouldn't have succeeded.

Sadly he nodded in agreement with his inner voice.

It was time to alert Abby and Tori.

He made his way to the mess.

The ladies were asleep, arms resting on the table, cradling their heads. They'd had a late night that lasted into early this morning, so he wasn't surprised they'd crashed for a few hours.

Tori woke the moment he entered and was about to rouse her sister, until he put a finger to his lips. She slid out the banquette and he slid in, taking her spot.

Before she left, Tori looked back, one corner of her lower lip caught between her teeth. Just as Abby did when she was concerned or concentrating.

Then they were alone.

"Liebchen?"

Abby stirred.

"The ROV is being hoisted on board with its collection basket full of gold bricks and a few small objects. Sigurd is showing his impatience."

Instantly she wakened.

He took in her swollen eyes, the tiredness drawn on her face, and he ached for her. But she was the one who needed to get it, to understand. There was nothing more he could do to make her see that her need for taking these risky challenges would kill her as surely as if she put a gun to her head and pulled the trigger.

“I don't know if Sigurd’s going to show his colors now, but I wanted to prepare you. Abby, you're exhausted. Perhaps you should stay here. I don't think the man will be able to take us all.”

“No.”

Her answer was as he expected.

Chapter Eighteen

What the hell was going on?

The gold bricks were fake, gilded to look like the real thing, but definitely not.

Sigurd clawed through the pile, tossing them aside as waste. The few pieces of Viking gold were small, inconsequential trinkets.

There were wooden shards from the crates preserved by the cold water of the fjord, one big enough to see part of a swastika burned into its surface.

So this was the right plane. But why the fake bricks? Who would have done this? Few people had knowledge about the gold transfer. His great grandfather would have made sure that no one in the Ødegård family survived. And as a high-ranking figure in the Reich, Hadrid Thorsen had the authority to either eliminate or relocate his underlings without suspicion.

Sigurd knew from his research that POWs from Norway and other countries had been brought in to build the submarine bunker Dora-1, and that there had been uprisings of those workers against their German overlords. Even a few Nazis were killed. His great grandfather would have used those incidents to mask the murder of his minions.

Sigurd's father had told him the plan had been for his great grandfather to steal the gold after it arrived in Germany, not for the plane to have a catastrophic accident before leaving the airspace of Norway. There had been an element here that no one knew about.

Yet.

Sigurd was aware that Reid was watching him. Even though he helped sift through the find, the man's gaze was always coming back to him.

The phone on his belt buzzed, and Sigurd looked at the number. Again, it was his lieutenant whose troops had messed up at the Cathedral. Maybe they'd found Catherine.

"Excuse me, I need to take this." Sigurd moved to the port side of the ship, keeping an eye on the last of the sifting work going on with the haul from the fjord's floor.

He'd make them take the ROV down again right after this call. Enough time wasted. He needed that medallion.

From the corner of his eye, he saw Reid signal to a crewman to follow him. It didn't matter, this was a report he'd be listening to, not a conversation. And the few words he would use were codes.

But the words he heard changed everything. He disconnected from the call and thought quickly.

The last of the haul had been sorted. It played perfectly into his hands. It only took another swift glance through the real artifacts to discern that the medallion wasn't among them.

"We need to meet in the mess and discuss this charade. It might be that Herr Weiss will not want to spend more money on hauling up fake gold bars," Sigurd said after returning to Reid.

Just then Tori came onto the deck and headed to the carefully stacked pile of golden bricks and the small pile of Viking objects. She picked up one and scratched the surface with her nail. "This is odd, don't you think?"

"Yep, we're heading to the mess to discuss it with Hermann," Reid said.

"He's still there with Abby."

Oh, this was better than he'd hoped. "I'll meet you there in a minute. I need to use the head," Sigurd said.

They left the deck together, Sigurd heading for his berth. He stopped by his bunk and pulled what he needed from his small suitcase. Then he headed back to the fantail deck and the pile of bricks. Picking up one, he studied it, pretending to show confusion when in fact things couldn't be more clear. He quickly did what he needed to do and set it down, placing other bricks on top.

Sigurd stood outside the *Brizo*'s mess, needing another minute to calm down. To remind himself that he wasn't going to fail. He had the upper hand. His troops were already in position. If only he'd had the information earlier that Magnus was the Ødegård, and that he'd been the one with Reid and Tori at the Cathedral's cemetery, meeting with the old man who'd been killed and the young one who had disappeared.

Sigurd could have taken them all that day. Swiftly and without mercy. Except for the Ødegård of course, who would have led him to the medallion one way or the other.

It would have been a done deal.

But the shooter who'd reacted with such bad judgment had fled the scene, knowing he'd made a fatal mistake. Which indeed was true. It had taken more than twenty-four hours to find him, get the information from him, corroborated by the digital images he took, and then kill him.

Sigurd fondled the equipment in his pocket, knowing his new plan was solid. No one would refuse to go along with it. He'd get Magnus, the gold and the medallion.

He took a cleansing breath. There was no one left to soothe him, to bring him clarity.

Catherine had been a great perk, but he'd get another as soon as he brought his task to fruition. In fact he could have any woman he wanted once he sat at the table of three. Any number of women and servants, and other SineQuaNon members would kowtow to him. The power and sway he'd hold would be immense.

Yes, his destiny was close at hand. He could taste the victory. The hell with anyone that got in his way.

Taking another deep breath, he entered the *Brizo*'s mess and faced the traitors within.

Chapter Nineteen

They expected trouble. Sigurd wasn't going to continue acting his part for much longer. Hermann and Reid had created an old-school setup of guns taped to the underside of the table. The mic on the TV monitor was turned on even though the screen remained dark. From his position in the Bridge, Captain Andrews could hear everything that went on. He'd know if there was trouble.

Hermann met Reid's gaze as Sigurd entered the mess. Their partner's eyes held an expectant gleam, but his attitude was relaxed. He smiled at all of them and glanced at the coffee maker as if deciding he wanted some. He filled a cup and headed their way.

Hermann noticed his hands were trembling as if nervous...or excited.

Placing his cup on the table, Sigurd spilled a bit and reached forward to mop it up. It took a second too long for Hermann to realize he'd used his left hand.

In a flash, Sigurd grabbed Abby, yanking her

out of the banquette. In a nearly instantaneous move, his arm was around her neck, holding her body tight against his. Hermann saw the glint of the needle before it sank into the soft flesh at her neck.

“Bastard. What did you do?” He tore the gun from its tape, jumped on the banquette and over the table, reaching for Sigurd. In another second Reid flanked him, gun pointed at Sigurd.

Tori moved so fast she was a blur and stood next to Abby, her arm around Sigurd's neck.

“You do anything and, regardless of how fast you are, I'll twitch and the rest of this goes in her.”

“Let him go, Tori. We'll do as he says,” Hermann said. She didn't move for a second and he couldn't blame her. She at least had her hands on the bastard.

Then she released him and took a few steps back to stand beside Reid.

“Right now,” Sigurd said, “you have ninety minutes to do exactly what I want. Then I'll give you the location of the antidote to save her.”

Abby slumped in Sigurd's grasp, but she still breathed, thank God.

“Put the guns in the dishwasher and turn it on.”

Hermann nodded to Tori.

She took the guns and did as asked. Then she returned to Reid's side.

“I want the medallion and Magnus in exchange for the love of your life, Hermann Weiss. The clock is ticking."

Only two other times in his life had Hermann felt this impotent. When he'd learned of his father's and brother's death in Viet Nam's Son Doong Cave, and when Abby had faced death in the Yucatan.

"Reid, the medallion," he said to the man beside him who vibrated with as much rage as he.

"And if you see the fine captain, tell him not to make a move after we leave. If you look out the window, you'll see six boats have moved closer," Sigurd said, a triumphant smile marring his face.

Reid ran up the stairs. And was back three agonizing minutes later while Herman watched Abby's breathing slow and her skin turn ashen. But as long as she breathed, there was hope.

Reid held out the leather frame to Sigurd.

"As you can see, my hands are full. Give it to Herr Weiss."

Hermann took the frame. His hands shook with fury. He needed to tamp down his anger and think, but that seemed beyond his capacity at the moment.

He fumbled with the two small latches, and he couldn't get the secret compartment to open.

"Show me the medallion." Sigurd's voice rose; he was losing patience. A bad sign for them all.

Hermann fought for calm, knowing all their lives were at stake, but for the moment, Abby was his sole focus. Finally the latch sprung open and revealed the medallion.

Sigurd's swift intake of air was audible

throughout the mess. “And a key as well. This is better than I'd hoped.”

Sigurd dropped the syringe and caressed Abby's neck while Hermann fought down the bile that rushed into his mouth. But he dare not attack the man. Sigurd had planned well. The antidote was his safe card.

“Okay, we move onto the deck,” Sigurd said. “Again, you rush me, you lose Abigail. That patch I just attached to her neck will inject the next dose if I push this button.” He held up a dead man's switch.

Two safe cards. He was better than Hermann had guessed. But then the SineQuaNon was known not for its failures but for its ruthlessness and cunning. Its failures simply disappeared.

Sigurd released his grip on Abby, and she fell in a limp heap to the floor.

Hermann's rage built to maelstrom. The bloody bastard would die for this.

Tori and Reid, followed by Hermann then Sigurd, exited the mess and headed through the short corridor to the fantail.

Hermann shook his head, and Andrews backed away, as did his men.

He couldn't stand that Abby was alone in the mess with whatever god-awful poison this lunatic had put in her. But he had to focus, find a way to save her. He wasn't at all sure Sigurd was telling the truth about the antidote, but he dare not risk having Sigurd push the plunger on the dead man's switch.

He alone climbed into the *Brizo's* own Zodiac while Sigurd waited on deck, still holding that damned switch, until a half dozen other inflatable boats reached them. Then Sigurd climbed into the boat. “Okay, on to Magnus.”

Hermann started the motor, glanced at his watch and realized ten minutes had already passed.

The *Brizo* was a long distance from shore. He pushed the boat's speed to maximum. As they bounced over the waves, he kept one eye on Sigurd, hoping the action didn’t jostle his finger down on the switch.

They passed the dock where the *Brizo* usually berthed.

“Where are you going? My car is parked there.”

“Magnus. It's faster this way.”

They led a small flotilla up the Nidelva River and docked at the last boat slip near a complex of apartment buildings.

***

The safe house Hermann had chosen was actually two apartments in a complex of modern, uniform buildings less than a half mile from the dock. There was land and water access, and to make it seem a less likely a spot to hide, there was a kindergarten in the development.

He rapped on the apartment's door with the knock code Magnus had suggested, then called him on the cell phone with the protocol they'd set up to indicate everything was safe.

Magnus opened the door and Sigurd pushed Hermann into the room.

"He has poisoned Abby and holds the antidote," Hermann explained quickly, not apologizing to Magnus for breaking his trust. There would be time for that after they got out of this.

"Yes, and she will die if you don't do exactly as I say. I know you're the current Ødegård and as such have power to control Odin's medallion. Thus you are in no danger of dying—for the moment. You must use the medallion to find the rest of the Viking's gold."

"It's on that plane," Magnus said, his confusion evident.

"No it's not. Where is it?"

"Magnus, there was no gold at the wreck site, or little enough to realize the bulk of it has been stashed someplace else. Despite the fact that the gold amplifies the power of the medallion, you are still the conduit. You are safe. Abby is not. In order for you to find the gold, I beg that you hold the medallion and see if you can sense where it might be hidden."

Hermann put every ounce of trust and promise into his gaze, praying that Magnus would understand his role in this. He, Reid, Abby and Tori wouldn't allow him to remain the captive of the SineQuaNon as long as any of them still breathed. *And if we don't succeed, Alfred will take up our banner and find you.*

Magnus blinked and nodded once. Thank God he understood.

Sigurd placed the medallion in the palm of his hand. As it had before, it jumped and his arm quivered.

Then nothing.

Hermann intercepted Magnus's panicked look.

“Think about what you want it to find. I think the gold we're looking for has some of the same gold from Odin that the medallion is made from.”

Magnus closed his eyes. Hermann saw his lips move as if talking aloud.

“Clock is still ticking.”

Magnus’s eyes flew open at Sigurd's warning.

“Keep concentrating.”

“I can't.”

“You can,” Hermann encouraged, countering Sigurd's abrupt orders. “Forget everything but finding the gold. He will tell us where the antidote is when we find it,” Hermann said, hearing the desperation in his own voice.

Magnus changed before his eyes. “I think Herr Thorsen should tell us where the antidote is before I do anything to help him.”

Hermann was stunned. Then he realized he'd miscalculated Magnus's fortitude.

“Give me your phone, Weiss, and yours as well, Ødegård. Then I will tell you, because until we find the gold, you won't get the phones back to tell the captain that the antidote is taped to one the fake gold bricks. Ironic isn't it? Easy to do as I searched through them. It's under their very noses."

Chapter Twenty

Catherine hadn't slept last night after escaping from the mansion. Every noise in the complex where the safe-house was located kept her awake. Her nerves were on overload.

The bed had been comfortable, but she was afraid to sleep, so she left the bedroom to pace the living space. The compact refrigerator had been stocked and the pantry as well, but the thought of food nauseated her.

She needed to get out of Norway, away from Sigurd and the SineQuaNon's reach. She had too much sensitive information about them in her head. But every time she reached for the phone in the bag Reid and Tori had promised was there, Catherine wondered if the two people whose numbers where programed into the phone were now in Sigurd's control. Calling them could bring her death.

All of a sudden an odd pattern of knocking sounded on the door. She froze, fear rippling up and down her spine.

Seconds later she realized the noise was next

door, which did nothing to alleviate her fear. For oddly, she heard a man that sounded like Herr Weiss talking in the hall. She'd only heard his voice during the dinner party at Sigurd's mansion, but she'd been trained to identify a person just from their voice and detect whether a voice held stress.

His certainly reverberated with tension. Something was wrong. Was he warning her by pretending to talk to someone next door?

She inched closer to the adjoining wall to listen.

". . . poisoned Abby and holds the antidote."

"Yes, and she will die if you don't do exactly as I say—"

Catherine's bowels turned to liquid. Sigurd's voice, filled with hatred and oddly triumphant. Had he found her? Was he toying with her?

She concentrated again and heard Sigurd gloat about where he'd hidden the antidote. Could she save the woman? And defeat or at least hamper Sigurd by doing so?

Minutes ticked by. Finally she heard the next door slam. Catherine watched the clock for ten long minutes, and hearing nothing else through the adjoining wall, pushed the button to call Captain Andrews, praying the call was in time.

Chapter Twenty-One

At first Hermann thought he'd heard wrong. The antidote that would save Abby's life was, as Sigurd boasted, right under their noses on the *Brizo*?

Then he realized it made sense. Sigurd needed a failsafe if they'd been able to inject him with his own poison. Hermann would bet the bastard left a note or instructions somewhere on his body.

Regardless, now he had no way to communicate the lifesaving knowledge unless they got to the gold in record time.

Magnus's eyes were squeezed shut, fiercely concentrating on the medallion in his hand while Sigurd's fingers, steepled at his waist, tapped against each other, the dead man's switch cradled between his palms.

The man was antsy, and Hermann prayed he'd lose enough focus that a chance would open up to kill him instantly before he could push the button. Then if he was right, he could look for the location of the antidote on Sigurd's dead body.

As if the medallion knew time was of the

essence, it started to glow. Magnus opened his eyes in surprise and folded his fingers around the metal as it seemed to want to jump out of his hand.

Magnus moved toward the door, and Sigurd opened it for him, motioned for Hermann to go next, and slammed the safe-house door behind them.

They left the building at a run. Magnus darted beneath the busy overpass, dodging traffic, heading toward the water, the medallion vibrating in his outstretched hand. Almost as if it were pulling Magnus along.

Hermann refused to look at his watch. He had to be vigilant in case Sigurd weakened for the millisecond it would take to jump him.

"It's taking us to the Archives," Magnus said as they approached the parking lot of the National Archives and, behind it, the hulk of the Dora-1 submarine base.

They passed both.

When they reached the end of the pier with nothing but the Trondheim fjord before them, Magnus stopped and stared at the medallion now sitting still in his palm. "It's gone."

"It better not be. You've got less than thirty minutes," Sigurd said. He pulled out a cell phone and gave instructions in a code Hermann had no knowledge of.

"Sigurd, you no longer need my assistance. Allow me to return to the *Brizo*. You can call in the location of the antidote as soon as you reach the gold."

"You're quite correct, Hermann Weiss, I don't need you," he said, sneering over the name Weiss. "But it's quite enjoyable watching you suffer, wondering what is happening back there. I can tell you the poison is well timed and that currently your fiancée breathes. But any attack on me and–" Sigurd held up the dead man's switch.

His lips twisted into a malicious parody of a grin.

Hermann forcibly unclenched his fist. Saving Abby depended on his vigilance in spotting that one second of opportunity when Sigurd's attention was diverted and he could be killed.

And since Sigurd was nearly euphoric at reaching his goal, he might let his guard down that one second needed. Hermann felt he had a good chance until those six inflatable boats zoomed up again. He bit back the bile that surged up his throat and refused to let another setback chip away at his resolve.

The man would die.

Sigurd motioned toward the largest of the three boats. "Get in."

Once on the water, the medallion began to vibrate again, pulling at Magnus's arm as if it were a spaniel pointing the way.

They rounded the pier and headed toward the bays of the World War II Nazi submarine base, Dora-1. The irony wasn't lost on Hermann. The Ødegård hid the gold the Nazis thought they'd plundered right under their very noses.

Three men in the boat stripped off their diving gear, laying the equipment on the seats of the boats. This wasn't a dry suit operation—it couldn't be that deep here, and neoprene with face masks and a single tank would be enough.

"Put on the gear, please."

"After you call in the location of the antidote."

"Herr Weiss, you only waste time. Put on the gear."

Hermann did as requested, realizing that Sigurd was right, the time for talk was over. The sooner the gold was discovered, the better chance they had. *Leibchen, I love you, you are my heart.*

Magnus slid into the cold black water first, Hermann next, and then lastly, Sigurd.

They turned on their facemask lights, and Magus held out the medallion. As had happened on land, Magnus was moving fast, barely kicking. The gold was pulling him toward itself.

They traveled less than a hundred yards when Magnus stopped at what best could be described as a concrete bumper dividing the multiple bays of the sub-base. Magnus directed his facemask light to a large metal door with a small keyhole. The shiny metal was untouched by the corrosive brine of the sea water.

Chapter Twenty-Two

"There aren't many bricks left to search. You're sure Catherine said the gold bricks," Tori asked, frantically turning over each one along with Reid and Captain Andrews. The rest of the crew, with the exception of the medic, remained at their stations at the ready. The medic stayed at Abby's side.

"We'll find it, Darlin', we will," Reid said.

"What if he lied?"

"Don't think that."

"The bastard doesn't care if anyone lives or dies, only that he gets the medallion."

"Tori, revealing that there was an antidote was the only way he could get Hermann to leave Abby's side. Hell, it was the only reason to have Hermann not kill him right then and there. And I'm betting there is one in case we did fight him and he got stuck with his own poison. I bet the antidote's location is in a pocket on him. It's here. Believe it."

Tori scrabbled faster, picking up and discarding the gilded bricks, praying that Reid was right about Sigurd. This was twice that Tori had to watch her sister be the victim of lunacy. This crisis wasn't of her making though, as her stubborn search for the Stone of Heaven had been. Nevertheless, Abby was in mortal danger.

There were only a dozen or so bricks left. Tori picked up one and felt something smooth and plastic on the bottom. "I think this is it. Keep looking through them just in case." She sprang to her feet and rushed the brick with its precious packet down to the medic.

He carefully cut open the packet of powder. "I have no idea what this is, it could work, it could—"

"Just do it."

She cradled Abby against her. Her sister's body was cold. So very cold. And limp, boneless.

The medic mixed the black powder with enough saline solution to be able to draw it into a syringe.

Reid and Captain Andrews entered the mess just as the medic was finished preparing the antidote. "That's the only brick."

The medic looked at them, then at Tori, who nodded. He swabbed Abby's inner wrist, inserted the needle into her vein and pressed the plunger.

Abby stiffened, then convulsed. Tori held her tighter, trying to infuse her with her own enhanced strength.

Reid kneeled beside them, wrapping her and Abby in his arms as if he too was trying to give them strength. The healing power of his love.

Abby opened her eyes. She tried to speak, but

words wouldn't materialize. She swallowed, and Captain Andrews held a cup of water to her lips, letting a few drops trickle in.

Abby looked at Tori and then laboriously turned her head to find Reid. She glanced at Captain Andrews and the medic.

“Hermann?” Abby croaked his name.

Tori met Reid's gaze across the top of her sister's head. Tori had to tell her the truth. And then tell her that she still was in danger.

“Sigurd has him, doesn't he?”

Looking down at her sister, Tori nodded miserably. Abby tried to move. “Stay still, there is another challenge we first need to solve. You have a patch on your neck, and Sigurd has a dead man's switch that will inject another dose of the poison, enough to kill you instantly.”

“Enough if I were not given the antidote, or enough on top of what I had in me before,” Abby said, her voice raspy.

Tori couldn't believe her sister was lucid enough to think this clearly. “We don't know. Nor do we know what happens as the patch is removed. It could trigger the injection.”

Abby reached up to touch the patch and Tori winced, afraid even touching it would set it off. Damn Sigurd to hell.

“Promise me one thing. Tell Hermann I love him. No matter what, I'll always love him.”

And before Tori could react, Abby ripped the patch from her neck and threw it across the room.

"Abby," Tori screamed. But instead of the connection between them fading, it grew stronger, and she knew her sister was going to survive this. The patch hadn't activated.

Captain Andrews crossed the room and picked up the deadly square with tweezers the medic handed him. "Secure this, and when we reach port send it in for analysis. It might be the SineQuaNon poison of choice."

Reid tenderly lifted Abby from the floor and carried her to the banquette. Tori watched them, knowing the bond between them had been forged long before she came on the scene.

"Wise and foolish girl." Exasperation and fondness colored his words. "Tori and I'll go find Hermann and, if we're lucky, kill Sigurd."

"I'm going too."

"Abby, we have to move fast. Hermann has to be crazy with worry over you. He'll not be thinking straight . . . " Reid let the rest of his sentence hang. But Tori saw that Abby got the gist of the idea.

"He'll be distracted by worry over me and not fully engaged in the battle."

"Yes."

***

Reid held her and Tori knelt on the banquette beside her. Abby was surrounded by people who loved her except the one person whom she needed the most.

Images played through her mind with lightning speed, and she got what Hermann had been telling her.

She finally understood that her need for new and extreme challenges was a way of validating life. Her life.

While always competitive, it was only after her parent's death that the mundaneness of everyday life became a yoke she could shed by pushing limits. Finding newer and shinier adventures, people, and places.

When Hermann had been severely wounded in China on that quest for the Emperors' Dragon, and his chance of pulling through practically nil, a small part of her had withered. Abby hadn't realized at the time that she loved the man. All she knew for certain was that once again something was being taken away from her and that it hurt.

Instead of backing away, the itch grew stronger in her to battle back the pain and fear and win. Nothing would hold her back. She was free to do as she wanted. No one had the ability to control her.

At the same instant those thoughts played through her mind, she also felt the immense vulnerability that Hermann felt when she took these extreme risks. And while she was terrified of losing her freedom, only in that moment did she realize that freedom meant nothing if there wasn't someone to share it with.

Now she, too, was stripped bare and left vulnerable by the thought of losing the person she loved. And she hated the feeling. As Hermann did.

She understood that love made you vulnerable,

but without it, life was only half lived. Ironic since she'd thought just the opposite since the age of thirteen.

This time the itch that drove her was to save Hermann and then find a way to meld their lives together and if possible, continue their work together finding the unfindable. Taking risks was part of that life, but the risks had to be agreed on. It had to be a true partnership. A bonding of two lives.

Tori and Reid had managed it. She saw it not simply in the looks and gestures of two people deeply in love, but in the messages those glances held. They were on the same wavelength. Sure, they were each still headstrong, but now they were able to compromise to make it work for both of them. They were stronger in each other than they'd been separately.

Yes, she got it. Hermann couldn't watch her destroy herself by taking risks simply to challenge the forces of death. And now she no longer felt the need.

Abby replayed the words Reid had spoken a minute ago: *"He'll be distracted by worry over you and not fully engaged in the battle."*

"If—*when* we find them," Abby said, "if I'm not at top form, I'll hang back so you don't have to battle on my behalf and Hermann can engage fully. But I have to be there and try."

***

Adrenaline surged through Reid as he followed

Captain Andrews down to the lower deck and forward to a small and well-hidden compartment at the bow of the *Brizo*. The space was barely big enough for one man.

Captain Andrews rummaged quickly and found a small object the size and shape of a cell phone. "This will track Herr Weiss. He had a chip injected under his armpit once we realized the SineQuaNon was involved. He felt that he might become a direct target."

Reid was about to protest that they all should have been injected but realized that wasn't the point at this moment. "Why him?" *And why didn't he tell us?* All food for conversation once this immediate problem had been solved.

The captain, not surprisingly, didn't answer as he handed him two small pistols.

"Guns won't work underwater," Reid objected.

"These will. They're mini harpoons. There is a compressed air cylinder in the handle, two shots per gun."

Reid shook his head, realizing he should have guessed Hermann of all people would have the gadgets to solve any problem.

"And these." Andrews handed Reid three small flashlights. Reid didn't comment, waiting for the captain to tell him why they would work in the darkness of the fjord's waters.

The captain grinned for a split second, understanding. "There is no spill light from the flashlight's lenses. The concentrated beam cuts through smoke or dust. In this case silt. They work. That's how he found Miss Carswell. That and a beacon he placed in her dry suit."

Found Abby? That was another question for later, after they were all back aboard the *Brizo*, safe.

Reid swallowed hard. This treasure hunter path he'd chosen hadn't been as difficult when he'd been single, free of the bonds of love. Now Abby was searching for Hermann, and he was about to enter what he knew would be a fierce battle. And Tori wouldn't stay behind.

"I'll get the wet suits to your cabins, along with the more usual gear."

Reid knew that meant knives.

Back in the mess, Reid swiftly showed off the gadgets and how they worked to Tori and Abby. Then he handed the small tracker and one of the guns to Abby.

"A tracker?"

"Hermann injected a chip under his arm pit," Reid said, voice neutral, watching her.

"Something is going on between Sigurd and Hermann, something more than just being SineQuaNon and the gold," she said.

"I think you're right. But that's for later. Gear up. Neoprene, as I don't think we're going deep."

In their cabin Reid helped Tori zip into her snug wet suit, then put on his own. He strapped his knife to the inside of his left leg, then knelt in front of Tori, prepared to do the same for her, when he paused.

"It's okay, I know how to use it," she said.

"I'm hoping you don't have to, but—"

"Hey, I'll have it if I need it."

He finished pulling the strap taut, then stood and brushed her lips with his. The same feeling of protectiveness flooded him as it had in the Yucatan. "I love you, Tori Carswell Hunter. Don't be a hero this time, okay?"

"Same goes for you, Reid Hunter. Promise?" She smiled brilliantly, telling him they needed to be strong for each other, Abby, and Hermann.

He nodded, matched her smile and swallowed past the thickness in his throat.

They joined Abby in the bowels of the ship below the water line, and Andrews led them to an airlock. "This will drop you beneath the ship, so the other ships that Herr Thorsen has positioned around us won't see you depart. There are two DPVs in the chamber—"

"DPVs?" Tori asked.

"Diver Propulsion Vehicles," Reid answered. "They'll get us to wherever we're headed fast and save our energy."

"You know how to use one?"

"We've used them before. I'll have you ride with me, and Abby can drive her own." He glanced over at Abby to see her nod. "Okay, let's move."

Abby went first as there wasn't room for all three of them and the DVPs in the chamber. They heard the chamber flood when the water entered, then the swoosh of air as it re-pressurized. Abby was in the fjord beneath the boat waiting for them.

"Our turn. You okay with this?" Reid asked, knowing Tori had pushed herself to the limit battling the underground tightness of the cenote river last year. He feared this might be too much too soon for her.

"As long as I've got you beside me, I'll be fine."

He wanted to kiss her, but time was ticking away. They pulled down their masks, got the tanks flowing and gave a thumbs up to Captain Andrews.

Again, the chamber flooded quickly. Reid carefully watched Tori, and though her eyes were opened as wide as they would go, and her air bubbles were copious as she breathed quickly, she seemed okay. Then the door on the hull of the ship opened. They swam out and met Abby.

As he turned on the DPVs, Reid felt Tori grab onto his thigh. He gave her a couple of seconds to tuck her head behind his tanks as he'd instructed her.

Then he and Abby throttled up their rides and moved quickly away from the *Brizo*. The lights mounted on their masks made the going easier, and the flashing beeps led them to Hermann.

Chapter Twenty-Three

Sigurd handed Hermann the small key.

As he had trying to open Magnus's frame, Hermann again fumbled getting the small key into the lock. The last thing he needed was to drop it and waste precious time hunting through the silty channel bottom.

Biting down on his regulator mouthpiece, Hermann concentrated, steadied his hand and slid the key home.

The vault door swung open easily, revealing an opening that was tall and wide enough for a man to swim through and into the room.

Hermann moved his head to play his facemask light around the inside of the concrete chamber built into the sub base. He'd love to know how they got it done under the watchful eyes of the Nazis. But great need triumphed almost any obstacle.

Shallow rectangular metal trays were stacked carefully on top of each other, five high. There were at least ten stacks of five by five rows in the chamber.

Hermann glanced at Sigurd. The lens of the

mask distorted his eyes, but even so they gleamed with maniacal zeal.

Within minutes, divers from the other Zodiacs Sigurd had summoned joined them at the underwater vault, forming a line similar to a bucket brigade as the diver inside the room handed tray after tray out of the underwater tomb to waiting hands. The men swam them up to the surface and the boats, then returned to get in line for another tray.

Faster. Faster. The only way Sigurd would give Hermann the antidote's location was when this was over. During the transfer of the gold, Hermann had nothing to do except recognize that Abby could die through no rash activity of her own.

And so his worst nightmare would come true. To have thrown down the gauntlet to make her choose between him and her need was pigheadedly stupid. True, he didn't want to watch her take risks that weren't necessary. But he'd rather have her beside him so he could at the very least try and protect her. It was infinitely preferable to living without her.

If that meant giving up all this, he'd do it, no regrets.

Hermann also figured Sigurd wasn't stupid and would realize that if Abby died, he'd have to create a plan to kill everyone aboard the ship. Even if only one of them survived, that one would hunt Sigurd relentlessly and extract vengeance. He'd always be looking over his shoulder.

The diver inside the chamber swam out, palms up. Sigurd had efficiently emptied all the gold.

Sigurd easily plucked the medallion from Magnus's palm. A diver, who Hermann assumed was a bodyguard, swam next to Magnus, watching as the medallion changed possession. At Sigurd's signal, he grasped Magnus's hands and bound them behind the dazed man. Magnus recovered enough to put up a futile struggle and the medallion glowed in Sigurd's hand as if in protest. But the bodyguard was able to swim Magnus up to the surface, probably to one of the inflatable boats.

The other divers followed, leaving Hermann and Sigurd alone in the black, silt-filled water.

It was the moment he'd been looking for.

He didn't have a knife or other killing tool at hand, but no matter, he had his fists and his fear.

With fury and adrenaline driving him, Hermann pushed off the wall of the underwater bunker and rammed Sigurd, pulling at his air tank tubes, yanking the regulator out of his mouth.

Grabbing one of Sigurd's arms and then the other, Hermann held them behind his back in a viselike grip.

Sigurd kicked backward, making contact with Hermann's legs and groin, but Hermann had the superior strength and hatred in his blood.

Then a bright light flashed in front of Hermann's eyes, instantly followed by shooting pain in the exposed skin of his neck.

The body guard had returned.

Sigurd's face dimmed as the darkness of unconsciousness engulfed Hermann.

His last coherent thought was of Abby, on the porch of their Oregon house, smiling with the smile reserved only for him.

Chapter Twenty-Four

The pings coming from Hermann's tracker implant grew stronger at the same time Abby caught the phosphorescent glint of churned water above them. She immediately slowed down her DPV and switched off her mask lights. "Go dark," she said urgently, thankful they had full-face dive masks with communication gear built in.

With their lights off, the water turned inky back.

"Look up. I think it's propeller churn. But oddly the signal for Hermann is still pointing ahead."

"How do you feel?"

"Strong, Reid. Fiercely strong. How about you and Tori go for the boats and I follow the signal?"

"Done. Be safe. Don't be stupid, Abby. SOS if you need help."

"No worries, I understand."

Not willing to risk alerting anyone on the surface by turning on her lights, Abby powered up her DPV and followed Hermann's signal, nearly crashing into a cement bulwark in the pitch black water.

Where in the hell are we?

The beeper glowed stronger. She let go of the vehicle, knowing it would stay where she left it, and swam around the obstacle, her hand on the cement, thinking it had to be a buoy weight. But the structure kept on in a straight line, so it had to be a pier piling or breakwater.

Worse, Hermann's signal strength grew fainter the farther she followed the bulwark.

Quickly backtracking, the signal showed her she was in the correct spot. Risking alerting Sigurd's troops, she switched on her face-mask lights.

And recoiled in horror when she realized there was a locked door built into the cement.

Hermann must be behind it.

The key! They'd wondered what it fit.

"Reid, we've got to get the key Magnus had. I'm certain Hermann is locked in a chamber, underwater."

***

"Damn." Reid didn't bother disguising his fury.

"Abby, I'm going to surface to see what's going on. Tori, I'm going to disconnect from the DPV, and I want you to stay here. Hold the grips, and it'll keep you afloat. When I head back down, I'll use the focused beam light. I won't lose you."

"I'm coming with you."

Reid thought that's what his new wife would say, and already had a plan. "Okay. Then we're going to surface together, but not stay up long. Keep your back to mine, and get as much info as you can, then we're down. Ten seconds, tops."

He felt Tori let go of his thigh, then disconnected his harness from the DPV, which floated exactly where it was. Thankfully they weren't more than twenty to twenty-five feet deep, so it took them no time to reach the surface.

What he saw wasn't encouraging. Six large inflatables moving out of the channel toward open water. Each filled with at least three men.

And in the midnight sun of late summer, he saw Sigurd standing at the bow of the lead boat.

He heard Tori's gasp. "We're at Dora-1!"

Turning quickly he saw the hulk of the submarine base in front of him. Hermann was locked somewhere in that?

Crap. Once again he, Tori and Abby were outnumbered as they had been in the Yucatan, but this time they had the element of surprise going for them.

He tugged Tori down beneath the surface and just as he was about to use the dive-mask mic again, he felt a black presence swim beside him. Reid turned, finger on the harpoon trigger, and at the last moment realized it was Abby with her DPV.

"Jeeze—"

"We've got to hurry—I have no idea if he has any tanks. He could be . . . " Abby trailed off.

"He's not. Don't think that," Tori said.

Reid planned fast. "Okay. We have four

harpoons. I'm going to shoot one at Sigurd's boat, see what I can do to slow them down, get them all in the water. His crew isn't leaving without him. If that works, you two go after Sigurd and Magnus. I'll work on the others."

"But—" Tori objected.

"Darlin', it'll work, trust me."

He didn't have time to say anymore. Pushing the DPV's motor to its max, he chased the lead boat's foamy white churn. When he was ten feet astern, he fired the gun. A bullet shot out, the casing dropped away and a multipronged, piercing harpoon struck and embedded itself deep into the boat's rubber pontoon.

Air bubbles flooded into the water.

Wrapping the trailing line attached to the harpoon gun around the grip of his DPV, Reid revved the motor and headed toward the old Nazi sub base, hoping to tear a big hole in the rubber of the boat.

Sure enough it worked, and the boat began to sink. "Got it! Abby, can you take Sigurd?"

"Still feeling strong."

"Okay, I'll take care of these guys and be with you as soon as I can. Tori, find Magnus and get him on land. See if he can use the medallion to help us. Go!"

Chapter Twenty-Five

Minutes were ticking by too fast. Abby's gut clenched in fear, but the only thing she knew to do was keep fighting and hope Hermann would live. Giving in wasn't an option.

"Hold on, Tori. I'm going in fast," Abby said. "When we get close enough to Sigurd to do some damage, I'll disconnect myself from the DPV and give it to you. Use the trigger on the right handle, press it twice quickly and it'll be at full power. Trigger it again and it'll go off. Got it?"

"Yes."

"Get Magnus onto the pier. I saw a ladder about one hundred yards back. Sigurd won't risk killing him, with or without the medallion." Abby felt her twin grab her leg, telling her she was tucked in place and ready to go. "Turn on your lights."

She throttled up the machine and headed as deep as possible, then toward the sinking craft. Even in the inky water their facemask lights made it easy to spot Magnus and Sigurd swimming away from the wreck.

Abby tried to push back her anxiety over

Hermann and concentrate solely on Sigurd as Tori had to focus on getting to Magnus and not worry about Reid fighting the rest of the boat's crew while utterly outnumbered.

Abby saw that neither Sigurd nor Magnus wore their fins, belatedly realizing that wearing them in the Zodiac would have been impossible. Their lack of fin power gave her team a hefty advantage.

Abby pulled the DPV within two lengths of Sigurd, slowed the vehicle to a crawl and let go. She didn't look back at Tori, knowing her twin would be fine as long as Abby kept Sigurd occupied . . . or he died.

Pulling the harpoon gun from its holster, she aimed at Sigurd's tank and squeezed the trigger, not blinking for a second. The harpoon tore into the metal.

She had him.

Finning as hard as she could, Abby towed Sigurd behind her and headed toward the pings and Hermann's underwater locker. The bastard would unlock the locker or die.

Then the line went slack. Glancing back she saw the slack harpoon cable trailing in the water behind her.

Whirling around, she saw lights coming toward her, and the silhouette of a diver swimming perpendicular to the lights.

Sigurd.

Damn. Abby realized that Tori's mask lights were a beacon to the bastard. There was no other way for Tori to find the ladder but use her lights, but the same illumination also marked her as a target. Worse, Magnus was with her, so the Ødegård and the SineQuaNon would be joined once again.

Sigurd couldn't be allowed to reach Tori and Magnus before she did. Abby took two seconds and pulled her lethally sharp knife from the scabbard on her inner left leg.

Then, finning as hard as she could, she chased Sigurd.

Tori, with the power of the DPV, reached the ladder first, and waited until Magnus climbed to the surface, then quickly followed him, leaving the DPV floating by the ladder.

Sigurd reached the ladder and started climbing. One last hard kick and Abby reached him, grabbed his ankle and pulled, stopping him.

He released one hand from the ladder to cover the zippered left pocket of his wetsuit. The area pulsed as if his heart were beating out of his chest.

Sigurd was trying to protect whatever was in that pocket, and she realized it was the medallion. It looked as if it was trying to escape its neoprene confinement.

Risking letting go, she kicked upward and was face to face with Sigurd. His lips pulled back in a snarl as his teeth clenched the mouthpiece. Hatred blazed from his eyes behind his mask.

She felt exactly the same way.

Abby slashed the pocket. The small circle of

gold burst from the torn neoprene and flew upward. Sigurd grabbed at it and lost his balance, falling sideways at her. Tumbling backward, they became a tangle of tanks, arms, and legs, the water slowing their movements. Then Abby saw Sigurd reach downward toward the dive knife strapped to his thigh. She couldn't disengage from him fast enough.

The skin of her right shoulder separated and blood swirled in the water around her. Her arm numbed and she dropped her knife.

“Damn,” she howled in frustration and pain. Forgetting everyone could hear her.

Sigurd grabbed the DPV Tori had left by the ladder and hit the throttle.

“Abby?” Reid asked through the mic, voice filled with alarm.

“He got my arm. I'm okay, Reid. He took the DPV and has a head start. I'm following him. He's heading for one of the boats.”

Just then the water lit with an explosion. The shockwaves pulsing through the water pushed her back toward the ladder.

The waves also pushed Sigurd away from his target, one of the four remaining Zodiac boats.

“What was that?” Abby said into her mic.

“Jesus, what the hell was that?” Reid's voice sounded in her ear a millisecond later.

“Magnus,” Tori said. “He used the medallion to blow up one of the boats. He says he can blow open the vault door.”

"Tell him to wait—he might blow up Hermann as well," Reid said.

Abby's heart sank. Reid was right.

"Does Magnus know where the key is?"

"Sigurd has it around his neck."

Four more explosions in rapid succession. The light was unbearably bright in the water, and the concussion running through the water stopped Abby dead.

Moments passed. The intense light faded and pressure waves in the submarine channel diminished.

"Now Sigurd is heading back to the dock. Tori, get Magnus out of there."

"He's not leaving and I'm not leaving him."

"Darlin', I'm heading your way," Reid said. "There aren't any survivors in the water."

"I'm heading there too." Abby finned hard, but her mask lights showed she was too late.

Sigurd was climbing the ladder up to the dock.

***

The numbness in Abby's arm had worn off, replaced by intense, jagged pain. She reached the ladder, hooked her ruined arm through one of the rungs, and pushed off her fins with her good left arm, letting them drop into the silt below. Then she turned off her facemask lights.

Climbing the slippery ladder one-handed was agonizingly slow. Finally she breached the surface and reached eye level with the cement surface of the pier.

Tori faced the ladder, wielding her own dive knife, her dive mask on the ground next to her, ready to lunge at Sigurd.

Magnus stood behind her, his hand outstretched, the medallion glowing brightly in his palm.

Sigurd paused in front of them, palms up, arms reaching toward them.

A terrifying tableau.

Tori's lips were moving, but Abby still wore her dive mask and couldn't hear. Clenching her thighs around the narrow ladder to hold her steady since her right arm was useless, she disconnected her dive mask and let it drop to the bottom of the fjord.

"Blow me up and you lose the key. Fair exchange, I say. The key for the life of Hermann Weiss, the medallion and the Ødegård for me," Sigurd said.

Abby thought quickly, realizing she had one chance to take out Sigurd. A poor one, since she had to use her left hand, but there wasn't another choice until Reid reached them. And Abby was pretty sure it was all going to hell in the next few seconds and that he wouldn't get there in time.

She fought to ignore the searing pain in her right arm and clenched the barrel of the harpoon gun in her teeth. Then she grasped the handle of the ladder and moved up one step. Once again she squeezed the ladder with her thighs for support so she could let go of the rung and use her left hand to shoot.

The midnight sun offered enough light for her movement to be noticed by Tori, who automatically looked in her direction.

Sigurd turned slightly to follow her glance and at that moment, Abby grabbed the handle of her gun, unclenched her teeth from the barrel, and whipped it toward Sigurd. Taking split-second aim, she fired.

At this close range and without the resistance of water, the harpoon struck Sigurd at full speed and buried itself deep in his side.

He fell to his knees, then pitched forward, his arms keeping him from face-planting onto the cement.

Blood poured from his wound. A mortal hit, but not the instant death she was hoping for.

Sigurd reached up toward his neck.

"Grab the key," Abby yelled. Before Tori could react, Sigurd yanked off the cord and threw it, with the small key attached, into the dark water.

Abby pushed backward off the ladder into the fjord.

She had nothing but fear and love helping her. No facemask with lights and no fins to help propel her downward to find the key.

***

The water was dark and Abby's facemask with lights and regulator was somewhere down below, but her buddy regulator was still available. Fumbling for it, her lungs squeezed for air, she found it, stuck it in her mouth and breathed.

Then she remembered the flashlight Reid had given her from Hermann's locker of gadgets. It had no spill light, and the beam would cut through the silt suspended in the water.

But where to search?

Abby pushed her panic aside. She had no idea whether Hermann lived, but she had to believe he did. The alternative would freeze all thought and action.

She slowed her breathing and cleared her mind so she could play back the image of Sigurd as he tossed the key. She saw the arc of the cord, the small splash as it hit the water, and rapidly calculated the distance. It wasn't far, maybe thirty feet toward the sub base, and it hadn't arced far over the water—maybe five feet from the concrete pier that held Tori, Magnus and, hopefully, a dying Sigurd.

Still time ticked away and she must get to Hermann.

Closing in on the area she'd calculated, Abby fanned the silt. It bloomed around her, but the flashlight's beam cut through the murkiness and she could see the area bottom clearly. She played the light, left and right, methodically covering as much bottom ground as she could.

It was taking too long.

Then something glowed about five feet in front of her. Swimming toward it, she fanned the silt away and found the key.

Magnus must have been able to use the

medallion to concentrate on the key.

Tucking the precious cargo into the neck of her wetsuit, she checked the blinking beacon and headed for Hermann. Without fins it was going to take longer and use the last of her reserves. She had no idea how she was going to lift Hermann to the surface with her useless right arm, but she'd figure that out once the vault was open.

The water in front of her was suddenly lit. Turning her head she saw Reid right behind her on his DPV. She handed him the tracker and grabbed hold of his thigh as he revved up the vehicle and they cut through the water at maximum speed.

Chapter Twenty-Six

As Reid came up quickly behind Abby, he'd seen the damage Sigurd did to her arm. It was a nasty, deep cut. He'd bet there was nerve and muscle damage, plus a huge loss of blood. He was surprised she had any strength at all.

But then he knew the power of love. The incredible strength it gave when fighting for the one you cherished above all else. He knew Abby would keep going until Hermann was found.

Reid had worried when he lost communication with both Tori and Abby. He pushed the little underwater scooter as fast as it would go to locate the ladder Abby told Tori to use.

Finally Tori had put on her mask with the embedded communications gear and told him briefly what happened and where Abby might be.

Once near the ladder, he'd seen the beam from the flashlight and then the glow of the key. He turned the DPV toward Abby and now they were headed to the vault.

They still had plenty of air but he had no idea about Hermann or what they'd find once they opened the vault. If he had tanks, if they had air. If. If. If.

They reached the cement bunker. Abby pulled the cord from her wet suit and fumbled with the key, failing to get it into the lock.

She handed it to Reid. He inserted the key, and the lock turned easily. He swung the door open.

Hermann lay at the bottom of the bunker, absolutely still. No bubbles coming from his regulator.

Reid didn't look at Abby, knowing he'd see pure terror on her face. Wasting no time, he pulled Hermann out of the vault, and laid him across the DPV. He throttled the machine up, heading straight for the surface.

Abby didn't hold on to him, but swam up beside it, knowing the vehicle didn't need her extra weight to hold it back.

***

There wasn't time to get them to a solid deck, so Reid held the DPV against the bunker at the water's surface with Hermann stretched across the machine.

Abby pulled off Hermann's facemask and breathed into his mouth.

His face was gray, and so cold. She tried to find a pulse, but couldn't.

"Come on, my German, breathe, dammit, breathe."

"I finally figured it all out and you're not quitting on me," she said between breaths and through the tears that mingled with the water dripping from her face. Abby wanted to say all the things she knew Hermann needed to hear from her. But she couldn't talk and breathe, so she breathed.

She held two fingers against his wrist. "I still don't feel a pulse, Reid."

Abby tried unzipping his wetsuit so she could hit his chest, anything to get a heartbeat. But she couldn't float and hit with only one functioning arm.

Thankfully Reid knew exactly what she was thinking as he moved her hand out of the way and did it for her. She kept breathing for Hermann as Reid pounded his chest with his fist.

"Come on, you stubborn sonuvabitch. Don't quit on us now," he growled.

Abby wasn't stopping. Heartbeat or not, she'd breathe for them both until she couldn't.

"Liebchen."

Her hearing must be playing mean tricks as she thought she heard Hermann whisper her name. About to bend over and give him another breath, Reid held her back. She glared at him, and he pointed to Hermann's face.

Wide-eyed, Abby stared at her beloved German. His face was pink and his lips weren't as blue. Then he coughed and nearly fell off the DPV.

Abby caught her breath and showered his face with kisses. "God, you scared me. Marry me, Hermann. Now. Tonight."

Hermann's eyes closed, but his chest continued to rise. He was unconscious, but he lived.

“Let's get him stabilized, Abby. Then ask him again,” Reid said.

Chapter Twenty-Seven

Strong search lights bathed them in bright white light. Abby panicked, thinking the SineQuaNon had found them. She shaded her eyes and was barely able see the *Brizo* at the far end of the submarine base bay, heading their way. Help had arrived.

The crew got Hermann up to the boat in an emergency basket and carried him into his cabin. That was the only time Abby was forced to leave his side.

The medic hooked Hermann up to an oxygen cannula. And shortly after the man began cutting away her wetsuit sleeve to work on her shoulder, Captain Andrews entered the cabin.

"Sir, good to see you back aboard," the captain said. "It was a wee bit tense there."

The respect she saw in Hermann's eyes was reflected in Andrews's.

"The boats Herr Thorsen had surrounding us fled shortly after the explosions started—"

"Magnus's doing," Abby interrupted for Hermann's benefit. "He directed the power of the medallion, and poof."

Hermann nodded.

"Ouch." She yelped and jerked in pain as the medic taped her torn skin together.

"Sorry," he offered in apology as all eyes in the cabin focused on his first aid.

"Not your fault," she said with a wan smile.

"It's pretty damaged, more than I can fix here."

"Got something to take the edge off?"

"Yep, as soon as I'm done," he said, pressing a bandage over the bloody mess.

Captain Andrews nodded his encouragement to the medic. Abby realized once again that Hermann really did have a stellar crew.

The captain turned back to Hermann.

"So, sir, in light of the fact we're clear of the SineQuaNon for the moment, we're running a modified plan B. The Zodiac is in the channel, with five crewmen and Mr. Hunter. We're ready to leave when you give the signal. Mr. Jones and Mrs. Hunter are onboard. Ørland Main Air Station is expecting us."

"Then let's move now, before the authorities arrive."

"Aye, sir. Lassie." With a touch of his hand to his brow, the captain left.

The medic maneuvered her arm into a sling and gave her a shot of Marcaine to help dull the pain. He then read the pulse oximeter on Hermann's finger, gave a thumbs up, removed the oxygen cannula, and left them alone.

Finally.

But now she was afraid to repeat her proposal and have him refuse her. So she postponed that discussion by focusing on what the captain had said. “You had plans?”

“Captain Andrews and I had four contingency plans. This, more or less, was one of them. I didn't know the gold was secured in the water—I thought it was either buried near the Ødegård marker in the cemetery or back at the mansion. I figured once Sigurd was taken care of, we'd get the gold. But now I believe Captain Andrews is going to have the men in the Zodiac retrieve as much of the gold as possible from the channel and put it back in the vault. Then leave before the authorities arrive.”

“Good idea. There are dead bodies in the channel, along with Sigurd on the dock.”

“How did he die?”

“I harpooned him.”

“Effective. Are you okay with—”

“Yes.”

He held out his arm and crooked his finger for her to come to him. Hope flared in her heart that just maybe it would be okay between them.

Abby sank onto the bed and scooted across the blue bedspread so she was nestled as close to Hermann as her shoulder would allow.

“Though we never planned on the water, the idea is the same. The crew can come back when the furor has died down and search the bottom of the channel for any remaining gold they might have missed. Nobody knows it's there, so nobody will look for it. Once it's all recovered, we can put it and the medallion into a vault I've already decided to build."

"To protect Magnus and his heritage."

"But it won't protect us; they know who we are."

Abby nodded and glanced up at the midnight sun shining through the portholes as they cruised past the port of Trondheim.

"Where and what is Ørland Main Air Station?"

"It's at the end of the fjord and will provide enough cover and protection until Reid catches up with us, then we'll fly to Copenhagen and have your shoulder fixed."

"You have a surgeon waiting already?"

"No. But once I ask, my friend won't refuse. As I wouldn't refuse if she asked for help."

No, Hermann would never refuse help to friends.

Abby studied him. His color was back and the last of the blue had left his lips. Her German was as tough as they came.

Thankfully the water in the channel had been cold, slowing his heartbeat to practically nothing, facilitating shallow breathing. She didn't know how long he'd been without air, but thank God they got to him when they did.

Despite the hope she'd felt only seconds ago when she'd snuggled next to him, she was still nervous to ask him again if he'd marry her.

Maybe he had heard her and had given up on her anyway and was just softening the blow by holding her.

And if he does give up on you, what then? A life without him would be unbearable, so she figured she'd just have to find a way to convince him he'd made the wrong decision.

"What changed, Liebchen?"

So he had heard her.

She turned in his embrace to watch his face as she explained. "Nearly losing you. Tori plain-talking to me. Reid making sure I wouldn't risk the rescue if I couldn't really do it, telling me in so many words that he didn't quite trust me. Maybe finally growing up," she admitted. This wasn't going to be easy, but Hermann deserved to hear it all. Then she'd wait for his answer.

He stroked her cheek and leaned forward to kiss her brow. Then he sat back and waited for her to continue, his hand lightly massaging her neck.

Her gaze glued to his, she swallowed once. "This is going to sound a bit melodramatic, but I realized there was nothing to live for if you died. Of course, throwing myself on a Viking funeral boat wouldn't be my choice, I'd go on with my life. But I'd be without the man who'd become my mate in all things."

He stopped his light massage, his strong fingers gripping her neck for a second, then loosened, continuing their lazy exploration. In those few seconds she saw the blue in his eyes deepen to the same color they held in the aftermath of making love. Hope flared brighter in her heart.

"Even before my parents died, I was competitive. I remember always trying to best Tori at everything, from grades to swimming to digging razor clams. Sometimes I won, other times I lost." She shrugged and winced, as the Marcaine the medic had given her wasn't strong enough to do more than take an edge off the hurt.

"When our parents died, the pain of losing them was so intense and I was so angry they were gone, the only way I could beat it back was to push myself harder, faster, deeper." Abby realized her words came in a rush, but she needed to make sure he understood why she'd behaved the way she did before and what had changed now.

"All of that meant taking risks. Soon those weren't enough, so I picked bigger risks with better payoffs. I was exhilarated beyond the pain and anger. The adrenaline became almost a drug. Would I win? Become the biggest? Would I even survive? It was the ultimate freedom, or so I thought.

"Then Tori told me she went in the opposite direction, nearly becoming a hermit so she wouldn't expose herself to the pain of loving and losing. We both were afraid but handled it so differently." Abby shrugged, then winced again, but bit back her yowl of pain. "She realized before I did that pushing love away was as futile as trying to follow a rainbow.

"I finally grasped that whatever time you and I have together is what we have. Whether we're separated by natural causes or because..." she looked down at Hermann's hand resting on her thigh. Her heart pounded as she summoned up her courage and again met his gaze. "Or because you leave. And I'd rather love you wholly, commit to you wholly, than live without you."

Hermann said nothing for a few heartbeats. Painfully long heartbeats. For the first time Abby didn't know how to read him. His eyes revealed nothing. His massage had stopped. She had no clue if her words had made any difference.

"Do you want to give up these quests, these adventures?"

Hermann's voice remained neutral as he'd asked the question. She couldn't tell what her answer would mean to him, to them. Abby took a deep breath and let it out slowly. All she could do was be honest.

"No."

"Neither do I. But no matter how careful we are, danger goes hand in hand with this type of work."

"So we plan as thoroughly as we can."

"The SineQuaNon won't leave us alone."

"Then we work on plans to beat them."

Hermann nodded once, precisely.

"Then, Abigail Carswell, will you marry me?"

"Yes. Now. This moment. Right here," she said, happier than she'd been since that fateful night of her thirteenth birthday.

"How about tomorrow?"

Her jaw dropped. "Tomorrow? We have to wait that long?"

"Liebchen, tomorrow is in about ten minutes," Hermann said and gave her a weary grin.

By God it was a beautiful grin. She'd been so afraid she'd never see it again. Or the way his intensely blue eyes crinkled at the corners. She moved so she could align her lips with his. Moving hurt like hell but was so worth it. She marveled at the way his lips felt on hers. Like a new beginning.

"If you're going to make me wait, can we wait in here?" she asked, putting a suggestive tone into her voice.

"Liebchen, I don't think your arm is up to it."

"I know." She feigned a pout. "But you can hold me, Hermann Weiss. Hold me forever."

"That I can do."

Chapter Twenty-Eight

Abby and Hermann remained in their cabin though the ship was docked at Ørland Main Air Station. Abby endured the pain but refused any narcotics other than another lovely shot of Marcaine. She wanted to be completely aware of the vows she and Hermann were soon to share.

Hermann was loath to leave her after he cut off the rest of her wetsuit. But he had to leave handling her hair and dressing her to Tori.

Abby kneeled at the edge of the bathtub and carefully bent over on her left side only. It was awkward and as her shoulder slid in the direction of her lean, she realized she needed to hold her left hand over the sling to keep her shoulder from moving at all.

She heard Tori climb into the tub, then saw her twin's toes as she carefully wet Abby's hair, using the spray attachment in the tub to keep the water mostly off her wounded shoulder. Then she felt the gentle massage as the shampoo bloomed into bubbles running down the drain.

"I can't believe it," Tori said.

"Why not, Mrs. Hunter. It's time. I was a fool. You pointed it out."

"Move a bit to your right," Tori said. "That way I won't soak your bandage.

The warm spray washed the last of the fjord from her hair.

"Okay, I think that's it. Your hair is squeaky clean. And why not, you ask? Because you never do what I expect you to do, but this time you did. You made the best choice possible."

Abby stood with Tori's help and allowed her to wrap the towel turban-style around her hair. Then Abby enveloped her twin in a one-armed hug, holding her tight.

"Hermann is perfect for me and I believe me for him. I know how you felt on your wedding day, and I haven't a single doubt left inside me."

Abby felt the wetness on her cheeks, realizing it wasn't from the shampoo. She loosened her grip on Tori and saw the same tears on her cheeks.

Tori brushed them off Abby's cheeks before wiping them off her own.

"Okay, enough water works. Let's get you primped and ready for the ceremony."

Abby sat impatiently as Tori dried her hair then twisted it into a loose braid that hung down her back. There wasn't a wedding gown, so she borrowed the only dress on the ship. A Hawaiian print, ankle-length, one-shoulder sarong courtesy of Tori.

Hermann wanted to stay inside the ship to say their vows, but Abby didn't want to use the mess—it had too many memories. So they compromised and would say their vows topside but in the shelter of the bridge.

A tingle ran up Abby's spine that had nothing to do with Hermann gently holding her against his chest as they waited for Captain Andrews to call them. She looked up at him expectantly and received a wide smile in return.

Before the knock sounded on the door, Abby flung it open, knowing who was there. "Alfred!" She hugged her mentor with her good arm, overjoyed that everyone she loved was here to share their vows.

"So finally we are to celebrate your marriage, Abby-*niū*?"

Abby nodded, tears of joy in her eyes.

Tori and Reid crowded into the small stateroom, and Tori was next enveloped in Alfred's hug.

Hermann and Alfred clasped hands; then it was Reid's turn.

Abby looked at all the people in her stateroom, and an imp claimed her.

"Alfred? I met the most charming woman last week. A Mary Bottomsworth? She seemed to know you."

Lo and behold, miracles did happen. A red flush crept up his cheeks, and he wouldn't meet her gaze.

"I told her we'd all have dinner once we got back to Oregon."

Abby winked at Tori, who got the message and smiled broadly.

"I would like that, Abigail. Thank you for arranging it," Alfred said with a formality that surprised her for a second. Then she recalled Mary's blush and wondered what was the history between those two.

Just then Captain Andrews knocked. "Sir, we're ready."

***

Abby waited while Tori preceded her down the short flight of steps from the stateroom to the *Brizo's* aft deck.

Then it was her turn. She paused after reaching the deck, taking in the tableau before her. Hermann stood with Reid and Alfred flanking him. Captain Andrews in his dress whites was in the middle, and Tori moved into place on the right side.

The *Brizo's* crew, standing tall and proud, lined the ship's railings.

Abby's heart swelled again. It didn't matter that she didn't have flowers or music or champagne and cake. It mattered that the man she loved wholly stood there with a grin on his face. The love in his eyes seared into her soul.

She walked the short distance, and Hermann stepped forward to lead her the few remaining steps to the Captain.

"I have my orders to keep it short and sweet," Andrews said, giving them both a beaming smile. "By the powers of my captaincy aboard the *Brizo* and my judicial standing in Scotland, it is my honor to perform this service. Do you, Hermann Weiss, take Abigail Carswell to be your lawfully wedded wife—"

"Yes, forever, Abby, you are mine," Hermann interrupted, squeezing her hand, gazing at her as if he wanted to devour her.

Captain Andrews coughed.

"And do you Abigail Carswell take Hermann Weiss—"

"I do. Willingly, for the rest of my life. I love you with all my heart."

"Then by the two powers vested in me, I pronounce you husband and wife."

Hermann carefully wrapped her in his arms and captured her lips in a kiss that promised forever.

"Come on, wife, let's get you to the hospital."

In a few hours, Abby would be in Copenhagen under the care of an orthopedic surgeon and her world renowned staff. Hermann's friend had postponed her vacation to handle Abby's surgery.

Tori kissed her. Then Reid kissed her and patted Hermann on the back, welcoming him to Club Married, and Alfred touched the area of his heart.

No matter what the future brought, and as Hermann said, it was bound to bring back the

SineQuaNon somewhere, sometime, Abby would face it with the people she loved most.

And her wonderful, breathtaking husband, Hermann.

The End

ABOUT THE AUTHOR

L.A. Sartor began telling stories around the age of four when her mother, at L.A's insistence, wrote them down and L.A. illustrated them.

As an adult she writes suspense and action adventure novels with a dash of romance, and screenplays—she's had a contracted adaptation!

She lives in Colorado with her husband whom she met on a blind date. L.A. loves to travel and thinks life is an adventure and we should embrace the journey.

If you'd like to be the first to know about her latest releases or other fun news, please visit her website, http://www.lasartor.com and join her mailing list, and she'll send an email confirming your request.

Warm Regards, L.A. Sartor

All of L.A. Sartor's books are available in paperback or digital at Amazon.

DARE TO BELIEVE

Searching the grounds of Highgate...

If her daughter needed five more minutes with her fairies and elfin friends, then, by God, Cate would give them to her.

Working hard to keep her pace slow, she walked the cedar path through the cool, dappled shade of the Aspen grove, to the turquoise swimming pool and back again. Twice. Until her patience was burned through.

"Okay, baby, I'm sorry, but we really have to go." Moving deeper into the shady grove, sure Haley would jump out and try to scare her, Cate reached the high wall bordering the estate with no sign of her daughter.

About to retrace her steps back to the mansion, she stopped as a flash of pink caught her attention.

Hippity Hoppity Lippity Loppity, Haley's precious pink stuffed bunny, hung upside down on an Aspen branch at the base of the wall.

Cate forgot to breathe.

STONE OF HEAVEN

Book One in the Carswell Adventure Series

Deep in the Yucatan jungle...

She avoided his eyes for a moment, knowing he was watching her, and scanned his body, moving down to his long lean legs, wincing at bloody mess on his bandage. His cargo shorts were torn, and his sandals muddied and scraped. He looked pretty beat up and needed a doctor for the wound.

His face drew her back. Reid's eyes were beautiful. Brilliantly green, intelligent, holding deep secrets.

Why in hell was she thinking these thoughts right now? They'd just survived a potentially deadly crash. And that's why, Miss Victoria Carswell.

"Come closer," he said softly.

After what she'd just been thinking? Maybe not such a good idea, but her feet moved of their own volition. Traitors!

Reid raised his hand slowly toward her face, gently touched her bruised chin. Then she felt things being pulled from her hair.

"Twigs," he said.

His voice held a tinge of amusement, as if he'd read her thoughts.

BE MINE THIS CHRISTMAS NIGHT

Bestseller #1 Amazon Holiday Romance

Book One in the Star Light~Star Bright Series

On a cold snowy night...

At Jenny's quizzical look, Annie told the truth. "That was my new neighbor."

"Seriously? Wow. What did you do to put a scowl on that gorgeous face?"

"Why would you think I'd done something?"

Annie grinned at her friend's raised brow. "Celebrate the season with lights? Be an author his son loves? Be a woman? I have no idea."

Jenny pursed her lips and started ladling out the cider, taking the job from Annie.

As Annie left the cover of the carport to mingle and enjoy the lights, she called back, "And he's a widower," smiling wider when Jen's eyes grew large and her friend waggled her brows.

Despite Jenny's obvious insinuation that her neighbor was yummy and maybe available, Annie had no intention of finding out. Josh was adorable, and she'd love having him visit, but Cole? Not so much.

FOREVER YOURS THIS NEW YEAR'S NIGHT

Bestseller #1 Amazon Holiday Romance

Book Two in the Star Light~Star Bright Series

On a cold snowy Christmas Day...

"Back to our living arrangements."

"Jennifer, I know you have two labs; the one where you meet clients and where your employees work is located in downtown Boulder. And then there's your private lab, adjacent to your house. I can sleep in the private lab, assuming you have something horizontal for me to sleep on. You get your house. Better?"

"Gee, thanks," she said in a perfectly droll voice. "And the floor is horizontal."

Laughter erupted. He couldn't help it. This woman was quick and she was funny. Why was she such a cold bird the rest of the time?

"Just need a blanket and a pillow." His stomach rumbled. "Can we call for take-out and start work?"

"Christmas, remember?"

"Yeah, sorry. We can start tomorrow."

"No, I didn't mean that. Take-out other than pizza might be impossible, especially with this snow. Actually I can cook, I just don't do it often. How about an omelet and all the trimmings?"

"Like bacon?" he asked hopefully

"And fresh bread loaded with real butter that when I broil turns brown and bubbly on top."

Brice wiped his mouth, afraid he really was drooling. "You're on. And please tell me that there is a horizontal surface in your lab other than the floor?"

"Sure, the desk."

Brice grinned again.

47953215R00178

Made in the USA
Charleston, SC
20 October 2015